SHE STOOD FACING HIM LIKE A DUELIST ON THE FIELD OF HONOR. . . .

Matt stopped in his tracks and stared questioningly. "What is it? What's wrong?" Then his gaze dropped to the videotape in her hand. "I knew the cut was still rough," he began, emerald eyes clouding with puzzlement, "but you look like it's the worst thing since *Attack of the Killer Tomatoes.*"

"I'd rather have seen just about anything than what you've got here. How could you do this? I trusted you and all the time you were just making a fool of me!"

Matt's own countenance began to harden. "Did you see the whole thing or are you just jumping to conclusions?"

"I saw quite enough. I'm going to show this to a lawyer! All you wanted was to sensationalize my father's life and drag my family name through the mud to advance your career. Well, you're not going to get away with it, not if I can help it. If there's some legal way of stopping you, I'll find it!"

"But you haven't even seen the whole thing!"

Sarah's mouth tightened. "You're awfully good at talking your way out of things, but you're not going to do it—not this time!"

CANDLELIGHT ECSTASY ROMANCES ®

SUMMER WINE

Alexis Hill Jordan

A CANDLELIGHT ECSTASY ROMANCE ®

Published by
Dell Publishing Co., Inc.
1 Dag Hammarskjold Plaza
New York, New York 10017

Dell ® TM 681510, Dell Publishing Co., Inc.
Candlelight Ecstasy Romance®, 1,203,540, is a registered
trademark of Dell Publishing Co., Inc., New York, New
York.

ISBN: 0–440–18353–7

Printed in the United States of America
First printing—July 1984

To Our Readers:

We have been delighted with your enthusiastic response to Candlelight Ecstasy Romances®, and we thank you for the interest you have shown in this exciting series.

In the upcoming months we will continue to present the distinctive sensuous love stories you have come to expect only from Ecstasy. We look forward to bringing you many more books from your favorite authors and also the very finest work from new authors of contemporary romantic fiction.

As always, we are striving to present the unique, absorbing love stories that you enjoy most—books that are more than ordinary romance.

Your suggestions and comments are always welcome. Please write to us at the address below.

Sincerely,

The Editors
Candlelight Romances
1 Dag Hammarskjold Plaza
New York, New York 10017

CHAPTER ONE

As she jogged along the beach, Sarah Kiteredge's running shoes kicked up little mounds of white sand. Without looking down, she was aware of the grains scattering in the morning breeze coming off the ocean. It was going to be a fine day, she mused, glancing at the line of white clouds scudding across the deep blue sky. At this hour of the morning, the air had a clean, newly washed smell. But no matter how pleasant the afternoon might turn out, in Sarah's mind it could never compare to the splendid solitude of the early hours.

It was the need for solitude that had brought Sarah back to her family's home on Cape Cod. And for the past four months, ever since March's bluster had departed, her morning run had become an important ritual. It was a time to clear her head and think about the day's projects—and also to appreciate the natural beauty that surrounded her, she thought, gazing with her artist's eye out over the Atlantic's rolling swells.

At that moment, a piece of strangely twisted driftwood caught her attention. And Sarah was careful to note its location so she could pick it up on her return. That was another great thing about the morning; before the summer people came to scour the beach, she got the best pick of what the sea had offered during the night.

But as Sarah's hazel eyes lifted once more, her brow began to furrow. Just like the last two mornings, she wasn't alone on the beach after all. A few hundred yards in the distance she could see the shape of a man. And from his superb build and easy lope, she guessed it was the same golden-haired runner who had passed her briskly on the two previous mornings. But this time she was behind him. And since she was slower, there was no danger of another encounter. She knew it was selfish, but she couldn't help resenting an intrusion on the beach at her special time. After all, she'd been getting up at the crack of dawn to have it to herself.

For the next quarter mile Sarah jogged on, letting the distance between herself and the intruder gradually widen. She had quit thinking about him when she noticed suddenly that he had stopped for a breather, his hands resting lightly on narrow hips as he looked out to sea. Sarah came to a halt then, too, flipping a thick, dark braid over her shoulder. She'd had enough herself. Turning on her heels she began to stroll back along the line of the foam-flecked surf. Now that her run was over, she had the luxury of dawdling, pausing regularly to examine interesting bits of shell and sea-polished pebbles. With pleasure she stooped and picked them up, rubbing her fingertips along their smooth surfaces, visualizing how some of those delightfully sensuous curves might be interpreted in a piece of her sculpture. For the past month she had been concentrating hard on getting ready for a show of her artwork. It would be the first time her sculpture would be displayed in a New York gallery, and for any artist that was a milestone.

She was musing about this when she spotted the piece of driftwood she'd fancied earlier. It looked almost like a sea horse with wings, she thought, stooping down beside it. There was more of it buried in the sand than she'd guessed, and after she brushed some of the damp grains from the silvery surface and started to lift, it was still stuck fast. She was so absorbed in her task that she didn't hear the light crunch of footsteps behind her.

"I see you beat me to it," a pleasantly rich baritone voice observed.

Startled, Sarah swung around. Just a few feet away stood the runner she'd been trying to avoid. Up till now she'd only caught fleeting glimpses of him as he passed her by. But now she was able to take in more details. He was really something, she had to admit. From a distance he'd been gorgeous, but up close he was downright startling. Her gaze traveled up from his sinewy thighs past his blue nylon shorts to the firm line of his narrow waist and then quickly up to his face. Though it was sinfully handsome, it was surprisingly pleasant—not perfect in the Hollywood "pretty-boy" fashion she'd learned to despise but intelligent and good-natured. His well-shaped lips were curved up in a friendly smile, and his light-flecked green eyes regarded her warmly. So warmly, in fact, that she suddenly became conscious that her own shorts and T-shirt, damp from her exertions, were clinging to her small, slender form. Irrationally, her discomfort was intensified by the conviction that he must be at least five years younger than she.

"I beg your pardon?" she managed.

His beguiling smile widened, and the corners of his emerald eyes crinkled. "I see we're agreed on our tastes in driftwood as well as the best time to run." He gestured at the still empty stretch of sand around them. "Not many people are willing to get up this early to have the beach to themselves."

Sarah took a step backward. Even though this guy seemed so outwardly pleasant, an early-morning encounter with a stranger was not to her taste. "You must have seen it first since you were ahead of me," she told him. "I'll give it up to you if you really want it."

He shook his head, and Sarah's eye was caught by the way the wind ruffled the thick golden locks of his hair. "I wouldn't dream of taking it away from you. But it looks heavy. How about letting me carry it for you?" Even as he spoke he was kneeling down beside her and grasping one of the driftwood wings. But the piece was still stuck deeply in the damp sand below the wind-dried surface.

Automatically Sarah reached to brush away more of the wet grit. But as her fingers touched the wood, so did his long, tan ones. Accidentally their hands collided, and the unexpected contact with his warm skin made her jump and withdraw her own hand quickly.

Aware of her out-of-proportion reaction, he rocked back on his heels and gave her a thoughtful look. "Sorry," he murmured, and then turned back to the task of freeing the little natural sculpture from its sandy prison.

"Really, you don't have to—" Sarah began. But at just that moment he gave a mighty tug. The driftwood jerked free and the unexpected lack of resistance sent him tumbling backward.

Sarah couldn't suppress the laughter that bubbled up spontaneously. He looked so funny sprawled there, his long legs thrust in the air at an awkward angle and his arms wrapped protectively around the weathered piece of wood.

When he heard her amusement, the expression of surprise on his face gave way to an answering grin. "Not very graceful, I'll admit. But it *was* effective," he pointed out, laying the piece of driftwood beside him so he could brush off some of the wet sand clinging to his T-shirt and shorts. In the next moment he was back on his feet.

Now that the piece was completely exposed, Sarah studied it curiously. "It's not a sea horse after all, it's a dragon," she exclaimed.

His dark golden eyebrows arched, and he gave her a quizzical look. Irrelevantly Sarah noticed that the long lashes below those brows were rich and dark instead of blond. Answering his unspoken question, she began to explain. "With that snout and those wings, it looked like

10

a flying sea horse before. But now that I can see its long, curling tail, it looks more like it's all ready to breathe fire. Don't you think so?"

He appeared to take the question very seriously and began to walk around the object, assessing it from every angle. "No. I think the tail's too long," he finally observed. "Would you settle for a twisted, flying alligator?"

"An alligator?" Sarah protested. "That's much too prosaic. This is a mythical beast if I ever saw one."

Her new acquaintance cocked his head and studied her with amusement. "And just how do you know so much about mythical beasts?"

Sarah was suddenly embarrassed. A very private person, she rarely opened up to strangers. And here she was prattling on with this young man as though they were old friends. "I'm the artistic type," she finally muttered, her expressive, low-pitched voice edged once more with coolness.

But her companion ignored the slight withdrawal. Kneeling down, he hoisted the driftwood easily and stood up with it cradled in his arms. "Which way is home for Eustace the Dragon?" he inquired mischievously.

That caught her off guard, and she shot him an incredulous look. "Don't tell me you're a C. S. Lewis fan, too?"

He grinned engagingly. "Maybe I don't look the type, but I enjoyed the *Narnia* books so much when I was a kid that I decided they'd be the perfect vacation reading; you know—an antidote to my job in New York.

"Job in New York?" she blurted. "I thought you were still in college."

The stranger gazed at her with quiet amusement. "I might have said the same thing to you. With those braids you look about nineteen."

Sarah flushed. It had been more than a decade since she'd seen nineteen. And it was impossible not to be flattered. Yet the remark put her a bit on the defensive. "Well,

I don't run around in pigtails when I want people to take me seriously," she pointed out.

"I know what you mean," he agreed. "Unless I'm wearing a gray suit and a pin-striped tie, I don't get no respect." He paused and looked deprecatingly down at his running shorts and sleeveless T-shirt. "But if I had my driver's license with me, it would prove I'm a ripe old twenty-eight."

"Well, I guess I'll just have to take your word for it." Sarah smiled. There was no reason to tell him that she was four years his senior, she thought wryly.

What did he do for a living? she wondered, too reticent to ask for details. With his looks and easy assurance he could be anything from an actor to an advertising executive. He might even be a lawyer. Although it was hard to picture someone so vibrantly healthy in the gray flannel suit he'd mentioned, she knew many of the summer people who came to the Cape were professionals seeking respite from desk jobs.

As he spoke, they had unconsciously begun to stroll in the direction of the rock-strewn cut that led up the sandy bluff that protected the beach. When they had gained the top, the stranger pointed to the left. A few hundred yards away stood a small, weathered cottage with dark red trim. "That's the place I'm renting. My name's Matt, by the way, Matt Lyons."

"Sarah Kiteredge," she returned, a bit hesitantly. Too many people around here knew she was Wallace Kiteredge's daughter. And lately she'd been approached by several reporters looking for a new angle on his story. Well, she had a new angle, all right. And that was precisely why she'd brusquely turned away anyone who wanted to pry into her family background.

But thankfully Matt Lyons didn't seem to know who she was. "Nice to meet you, Sarah Kiteredge," he returned pleasantly. "Where will Eustace be making his new home?"

"Oh, you don't have to bother. We're almost there." She pointed toward a much larger gray house with white trim, which commanded the hill along the road. "I can carry it the rest of the way."

But he shook his fair head. "No. Eustace is heavier than you might think. I'd better see him the rest of the way."

Sarah opened her mouth to argue and then closed it again. It was obvious that further debate would accomplish nothing. She cast her new companion a sideways look through a screen of thick, dark lashes. On the surface of things there was really no good reason to reject his friendly offer. But the fact was, she couldn't help feeling a bit nervous about letting him in—especially since she was alone in the house. And yet as he kept pace beside her up the gravel path that led to her side door, there seemed no graceful way to extricate herself.

"What a fabulous old place," he exclaimed, looking up to admire the twin turrets and widow's walk that topped the rambling Victorian roof line. "Considering what I pay for my cottage, this castle must cost a king's ransom."

Sarah paused, suddenly seeing the magnificent turn-of-the-century structure the way it might look to a stranger. It had been her home ever since she could remember, although some years her family had spent only the summer on the Cape. Her father had been born and grown up in this house, and it had been in the Kiteredge family for generations. "I'm not renting," she explained to Matt. "This is my folks' place."

"A castle for a dragon. That's a perfect arrangement." He paused for a moment, looking thoughtfully down at the natural wood sculpture in his arms and then shifting its weight slightly. "But what would your parents think about your bringing a dragon home?"

Sarah's expression didn't change. But suddenly the

breeze from the ocean that still whipped strands of hair free from her braids seemed several degrees colder. "My parents are dead," she informed him quietly. "They were both killed in a boating accident last summer."

There was an awkward moment of silence broken only by the crunch of their running shoes on the gravel path that led around to her studio door.

"I'm sorry," Matt finally filled in. "I didn't mean to pry."

"You weren't prying," Sarah told him, opening the battered screen door and gesturing him onto the small wooden porch. "You couldn't know."

Matt's green eyes darkened, and a brief expression of regret flitted across his handsome face. He knew all about the boating accident. Actually, he had raised the subject only because he wanted to hear what Sarah would say about it. But now he almost wished he hadn't. Before he'd contrived to bump into her on the beach, he'd been thinking of her as a good source of information about Wallace Kiteredge, the famous Hollywood director of minor westerns whose work was only just being recognized for its real genius.

But now that he'd met her and been captivated by her hazel eyes, his attitude had shifted abruptly. Though she was remarkably pretty, it wasn't the kind of superficial prettiness that you could easily forget. Despite her girlish appearance, there was a strength, a finely drawn beauty in her face that he already knew was going to stay in his mind. And suddenly he wished they might have met under different circumstances. A half hour ago, his motives had been clear-cut. Now he found himself wanting to get to know Sarah as much as he wanted to pick her brains about her father.

Because he was essentially a straightforward person, any sort of duplicity made him uncomfortable. But he knew, too, that if he gave himself away he would never have the opportunity of getting closer to her. And he wasn't just being metaphorical. She was looking away, and that gave him the chance to study her more closely. On the beach when they'd been talking, he'd only been able to show polite interest. But now he was free to drink in the smooth apricot contours of her bare legs and the firmly rounded curve of her buttocks beneath her white shorts. And he knew that when she turned back to him, there would be an even more enticing roundness filling out the front of her yellow T-shirt. His hand itched to reach out and touch the satiny skin of her neck, so sweetly vulnerable underneath those sable braids. But he didn't dare. Perhaps that would come later.

With her back turned, Sarah was unaware of Matt Lyons's thoughts. She was holding the door open so that he could enter her studio. It was a large, sunny room that had once been a solarium. But Sarah had converted it to suit her own purposes. A tank of acetylene and a welding torch occupied one corner. Large crocks of various kinds of clay stood opposite. Shelves of glazes and pottery in different stages of preparation lined the wall above them. In the center of the room was a large, plastic-draped shape on a low table. It was a three-quarter-size nude female figure Sarah had been working on. She had conceived it as a major piece for her exhibition. But lately she'd begun to despair that it would ever come right.

She turned to see Matt gazing with open interest at the finished and unfinished pieces of small sculpture some stoneware and some metal—covering most available surfaces.

He stood gracefully poised in a shaft of light from the window. His sleeveless T-shirt and runner's briefs had seemed perfectly natural on the beach. But now that he was indoors, she was suddenly vividly aware of how little

15

covered his body. She could see every well-defined muscle in his long legs lightly sprinkled with stiff golden hair. And the sun-browned skin covering his broad shoulders had the sensuous texture of a Greek sculpture. Physically, he really was remarkable, she thought, trying to convince herself that she was appreciating him with the detached interest of an artist. But the little shiver of awareness that tingled up her spine as her gaze traveled up the line of his strongly molded back argued otherwise.

Just then he turned, and her gaze jerked away guiltily. But he seemed not to notice.

"You weren't kidding when you said you were the artistic type," he observed. "Where are you going to find room for the dragon?"

Glad for a distraction, Sarah gestured toward a set of wide shelves near the window. They held an assortment of natural objects she'd scavenged, which included everything from shells and driftwood to gull feathers.

"And I thought I was a pack rat. You're world class," Matt commented good-humoredly as he cleared a place amid the jumble. "If I set Eustace here, he can look out the window and greet you when you come home."

Sarah couldn't help smiling. "Maybe Eustace can even play watchdog and scare away intruders," she ventured, striving to match his playful mood.

Matt set down his burden very carefully and then straightened and turned toward her with a surprisingly serious expression. "I hope you're not putting me in that category." He paused. "I realize I've intruded on you this morning, but I mean no harm to the lady of the castle. Besides," he added with a sudden grin and a quick gesture at Eustace, "I've already made friends with your watch dragon."

Sarah shrugged helplessly. There was no denying that. With a flash of insight she knew that from now on whenever she looked at the driftwood dragon she would remem-

16

ber the tall, fair-haired stranger who had carried him home.

"I'd probably burn my hand off with that welding equipment of yours, but I've always wanted to learn to work with clay," he was saying conversationally. "It seems like it might be the perfect way to soothe my city-frazzled nerves."

Sarah did not respond, and Matt continued his inspection of her studio. After peering into the room that held the kiln, he headed across the studio and took one of her small, curving sculptures off a shelf. Holding it up to the light, he admired its smooth surface.

"This glaze is almost the same color as your eyes. In the sun I can see flecks of gold and green glinting just below the surface like a forest pool. It's a magical color—full of mystery and promise." He turned then and shot her a direct look.

Sarah felt her cheeks begin to heat. Looking down, she nervously began to chip at the painted surface of the table next to her. Matt Lyons might look younger than his years, but this was no inexperienced boy, she realized. He knew very well how to make a woman conscious of her femininity. The way he had just looked at her had made her feel he wanted something from her, and she suspected that it was something she was not prepared to give. Suddenly a sense of foreboding took hold of her, and she wanted very badly for him to go away and leave her alone.

However, he was still prowling her domain. And now his attention was on the large, draped figure in the center of the room. Sauntering toward it, he reached to lift a corner of the plastic that obscured it from view.

Sarah reacted almost with panic. "Don't touch that. It's not ready to be seen yet," she informed him brusquely. "In fact, if you don't mind, I have a lot of work to do today. Thank you for bringing the driftwood piece up from the beach," she added, the formal, rather prim tone of her

17

voice at odds with the friendly familiarity of only a moment before.

Though she gave him a tight smile, her visitor was quick to detect the dismissal in her tone. "You're right," he agreed, dropping the edge of the plastic. "Time we both got on with our day. Maybe I'll see you on the beach again," he added.

"Maybe," Sarah answered noncommittally. After he had shut the door behind him, Sarah stood quietly in the now empty room, waiting for the echoes of his presence to die down. Usually she was able to get to work almost immediately after her morning run. But today she couldn't seem to make the transition. It was only after she'd downed two strong, black cups of coffee and showered and changed that she was able to focus on the tasks she'd planned for the day.

Last night she'd determined that her main project was going to be *Dream Woman*, the plastic-draped sculpture that Matt had tried to uncover. Gordon Wentworth, Sarah's agent and close friend, had made it a must for her upcoming show. And when Gordon wasn't trying to romance her, his advice was sound.

On her last trip to New York, when they'd been having a quiet supper after the theater, he'd brought up the subject of the show he was arranging for her. "Your nonrepresentational work is so free and spontaneous," he'd told her. "But I think we need to show the New York critics that you have the training to be just as expressive with the human form. You need to give them a technical piece that will knock their patent leather shoes off."

Sarah had giggled at the image, but she had known he was right. Somehow, she felt much more comfortable revealing her private vision through swirling shapes and textures. But after almost a decade of working to perfect her craft, she was a technically accomplished artist and wanted to demonstrate that ability.

18

Yet, though she'd really been trying with this figure, the quality she wanted to capture in it still eluded her. The body proportions had given her no trouble. Since there had been no model available, she'd simply used a mirror. The construction process had actually been fun, and she'd enjoyed the secret joke of knowing that the lithe, graceful young woman taking shape was actually herself—until Matt Lyons had tried to look at it. Then she'd felt a rush of embarrassment, though it was ridiculous to think he might recognize it. The face certainly bore no resemblance to her own—or to what she wanted it to be. She had tried to give it a joyful expression to match the abandoned pose of the body. But struggle as she might, her fingers never quite captured the look she was after. "Maybe it's just that I don't really know what I want," she muttered aloud as she unwrapped the figure and began to study it from every angle.

Rather than tackle the face again, she wet down an arm and began smoothing the already well-formed clay. Absentmindedly her hand moved to the front of the figure and began to mold the high curve of the breasts. There was undoubtedly something sensually satisfying about working in clay, she admitted to herself as her fingers coaxed a perfect roundness. And then she stopped. *I'm certainly giving this figure a lot of attention,* she thought. And then an unsettling notion struck her. It had been a long time since anyone had given her real body much attention.

Even before her divorce from Brad two years earlier, that had been true. He had been at best a perfunctory lover. And at first she had wondered what was wrong with her. It had taken her a while to realize that, like many Hollywood denizens, he subscribed to the philosophy that the end justified the means. Although she hadn't suspected it during his ardent courtship, his main interest had been her father's connections with the movie industry.

She had met Brad when he was teaching directing at

UCLA and she was an art major. And because she'd been naive and ripe for love at that time, she'd been blind to his real purposes. But there was no way her self-deception could have lasted past the first years of their marriage. His exploitation of her connections, his total absorption with his career, and his increasing neglect all took their toll on the fragile relationship. But still she'd been too proud to become just another Hollywood divorce statistic. She'd tried to make things work, until that evening when she'd come home unexpectedly from a class and found her husband in the arms of the ingenue he was auditioning for a part in his first big film.

Sarah's normally soft mouth tightened to a grim line as she recalled the painful scene. Just how were you to know, she asked herself, what a man was really like? She'd certainly been fooled by Brad. And for years she'd thought she'd known her own father. But it had turned out she hadn't known him at all. Sarah's hand dropped from the figure and she turned toward the window with eyes that no longer took in the scene before her. It hadn't been just marriage that had disenchanted her. There had been the love letters she'd found when going through her father's effects after her parents' deaths. They weren't from her mother, but from an actress named Marjorie Winter. And from only a brief inspection of their contents, Sarah knew that the two had been having an affair for years and that her father was almost certainly the father of the actress's son, Philip. The realization had made her feel sick, but she wasn't going to think about that now, she told herself firmly, clenching her small fist as she turned back to the frustrating figure in the center of her studio.

Maybe if she couldn't get the eyes right she could do something with the expression of the mouth. But as she began to smooth and shape the lips, her thoughts spun out of control again. When finally she looked down at the task her distracted fingers had been absentmindedly performing, her hand froze. She had set out to shape the figure's mouth. Instead, she had rubbed it into a blur and distorted the bottom of the nose as well.

"Oh, great," she muttered in disgust. This was all Matt Lyons's fault, she thought irrationally. Since meeting him, she'd been able to accomplish less than nothing. Somehow he'd stirred up memories she preferred to bury. She wished she'd never met him on the beach. And she certainly didn't want to make a habit of bumping into him—not if he was going to make a shambles of her work on such short acquaintance. She didn't want or need an involvement now—and especially with someone who could be her kid brother.

So, what are you going to do about it, she asked herself as she re-covered the clay figure, not wanting to look at the mess she'd made, much less think about how to fix it.

Sarah heaved a long sigh and pushed her hair back from her damp face. There didn't seem to be much choice. Since she wasn't going to give up her run, she'd just have to get up an hour earlier and finish on the beach before Matt Lyons appeared.

The first faint streaks of pink were lightening the sky as Sarah made her way down the path the next morning. Though the air was still chilled from the night, she was soon warm from her exercise. And as she ran, she had the added bonus of watching the golden sun rise out of the sea like a gorgeous promise. But even with this distraction, she kept peering at her watch and glancing back over her shoulder to make sure she was still alone. And when she climbed back toward her house, it was with a sense of relief irrationally mixed with disappointment.

She had deliberately arranged to be alone. Yet, somehow her thoughts kept straying to Matt Lyons. What would he think when she didn't appear at her usual time? Would he surmise that she was avoiding him? Or would

21

he even give her a second thought? Though she had invested a lot of time speculating about him, chances were he had probably forgotten all about her.

Yet, despite all her wise lectures, after Sarah had showered and put on a bra and bikini panties, she found herself moving to the bank of windows at the front of her bedroom that provided a sweeping overlook of the beach. Perching on the varnished oak window seat, she began to brush out the length of her damp hair while her warm hazel eyes studied the deserted shoreline. After a shower she often sat this way, looking out at the water while her hair dried. And so it was easy to tell herself that she was not interested in spotting a lone, early-morning runner. Still, when a figure appeared at the extreme limit of her vision, her hand froze on the handle of her brush in mid-stroke. Though the moving outline was too far away to identify, there was no doubt in her mind who it was.

She felt her heart begin to pound as she tracked the long, easy strides with which the runner was quickly closing the distance between himself and the beach in front of her house. Though she knew she should get up and go down to her studio, she couldn't seem to move from her high vantage point. And her eyes remained fixed on Matt as he drew closer and closer. If she'd wondered what he was thinking before, the question was much more insistent now. It was a strange feeling, as though she could almost read his mind. As he ran, he occasionally looked from side to side, and she knew beyond a doubt that he was looking to find her.

When he reached the sandy stretch that led to the cut, he stopped and stood, outlined against the water with his hands on his hips and the wind ruffling his thick hair, the way she'd seen him looking out to sea the morning before. Only now he was turned inland toward her house. And though Sarah was certain that the light reflecting off the panes of glass would make it impossible for him to see her, she suddenly drew back. After all, what if he really could spot her sitting there staring at him with almost nothing on? But when she'd left her seat by the window, curiosity got the better of her. Peering around the edge of the white curtain, she looked out once more. Just as her eyes focused on the place where he still stood, his tall body began to move forward. In what seemed like only a moment, his long browned legs had brought him easily up the sandy slope that protected her property. And he was walking straight toward the house, his gaze still firmly fixed on the windows of her bedroom.

CHAPTER TWO

For an endless moment as she watched Matt's progress toward the house, Sara stood frozen at the window's edge. It was obvious that he intended to knock at the door. And what in the world was she going to do? Her first impulse was to pretend that she wasn't at home. And if Matt had simply rapped gently on the door and then turned away, that's how it would have gone. But his first few polite taps were quickly followed by a more resolute hammering. Apparently he wasn't going to give up easily. And she certainly couldn't go to the door like this, she thought, looking down at her all but nude body.

Hastily she grabbed for the jeans she'd thrown on the overstuffed chintz chair beside her bed the night before. She was just yanking on a burgundy T-shirt when the persistent knocking stopped. She paused in the act of running her fingers quickly through her hair, thinking that perhaps he'd given up after all. But then she heard his voice at the front of the house calling her name. When she didn't respond, he rattled a front window. My God, was he planning on breaking in? The thought galvanized her into action.

Without pausing to slip into sandals, she ran barefoot down the stairs and tugged at the knob. Made of hand-worked chestnut, the ancient door was almost never used. And the summer heat had swollen it into its frame so that it refused to swing open. But Matt was obviously aware that Sarah was on the other side of it. She could see him cupping his hands to the glass of one of the living room windows and peering in.

Abandoning the struggle to open the stuck door, she turned in his direction and gestured toward the other side of the house. "Come around to the kitchen door," she called.

Giving her a thumbs-up sign, he quickly disappeared from view. And she started for the kitchen.

"I was worried about you," he explained as she opened the back screen a few inches. "You're not sick, are you?" Both the tone of his voice and the expression on his face conveyed his concern.

She shook her head, struggling to keep her own expression neutral. "I'm fine."

"But you weren't on the beach," he persisted.

His questions were making Sarah feel both foolish and uncomfortable. How could she possibly explain her odd behavior? And then inspiration struck. "I couldn't sleep worrying about a project I'm working on," she fibbed. "After tossing and turning, I decided I might as well get up and run early."

He cocked his head and gave her a quizzical look. "I missed you. Even though we just met yesterday, I've gotten used to seeing you these past few days, and somehow the morning feels wrong if you're not there."

"Oh" was all Sarah could manage. She couldn't think of how to answer him properly. What's more, he was standing on the porch with his long legs firmly planted as though he had no intention of going away. For lack of anything else to say, and feeling guilty about her deception, she found herself asking, "Would you like to come in for coffee? I'm just about to have some."

His tanned face broke into a smile. "That sounds great."

Pulling the door open, she watched him enter, thinking

25

to herself that the invitation was probably a mistake. But it was too late to take it back. Matt was looking around her old-fashioned kitchen with its outsize cupboards and long porcelain drainboard as though he intended to move in. "Those oak cabinets are real gems," he complimented. "I'm glad someone had the good sense not to cover them with white paint."

Sarah chuckled as she began measuring out coffee into the battered aluminum percolator. "That's exactly what my mother wanted to do when everybody around here was on a 'modernization' kick. But my father wouldn't let her."

Matt gazed at her with a surprisingly intent expression. "Sounds like your father had the right idea. What kind of guy was he?"

Sarah cleared her throat. "Oh, uh—a lot like me, I guess." Her withdrawn tone of voice made it clear that she didn't want to pursue the topic. There was a speculative look in Matt's eye as he studied her. And then, opting to abandon the subject, he pulled out one of the Windsor chairs at the round, claw-foot table and sat down. For a moment Sarah observed him in silence. Once again she was becoming uncomfortably aware of how little of his muscular body was covered by running shorts and a T-shirt. And then an amusing thought struck her, and her mouth curled in a grin.

"What's so funny?" Matt demanded.

"I was just wondering what you look like with your clothes on," she blurted, and then her hand flew to her mouth as if to call back the provocative words.

Matt chuckled. "Well, if I have anything to say about it, this is definitely not the only way you'll get to see me," he assured her.

Sarah paused while she thought that remark over and then turned quickly toward the coffee, wishing it would begin to bubble so she'd have something else besides Matt Lyons to command her attention.

"I picked some black raspberries yesterday," she told him over her shoulder. "I was planning on having them with my corn flakes. Would you like to join me?"

His response was enthusiastic. "Black raspberries. I haven't had them since my Boy Scout summer camp days. I'd love some."

Sarah turned to the refrigerator and pulled out the bowl of tart, glistening little pieces of fruit. Taking them to the sink, she turned on the water. At that moment the percolator began to bubble.

Matt pushed back his chair and stood up. "Let me get the coffee," he offered. "Where do you keep your cups?"

"Never mind. They're right here in the cupboard above the sink," she began, knowing that he would have to reach directly above her to get them.

But he ignored her mild protest. Before she could move he was across the room and in back of her, pulling open the doors above. "Now watch your head," he warned, touching her shoulder lightly. Sarah's hands seemed to freeze on the colander she was holding, and her body went rigid. She was intensely conscious of the heat of his superbly male body, only fractions of an inch from hers. And as his arm reached upward, the thick blond hairs on his forearm brushed lightly against her cheek.

Though it took him only a matter of seconds to pull down two thick white mugs, for Sarah the moment seemed to last forever. But as he ambled over to the stove and began to pour the steaming black brew, the world snapped back into focus. "Do you take cream or sugar?" he asked.

"Neither one," Sarah told him. "But I do like some milk." As she spoke, she set the fruit and a box of cereal down on the table.

A few minutes later Sarah was seated across from Matt, watching him spoon the wild berries into a bowl. The

27

morning light that spilled onto the table from the window seemed drawn to the gold in his hair. It washed over his face, highlighting his strong features and the texture of his skin.

"These are delicious," Matt complimented. "I'd forgotten how much better the wild ones are. Are you willing to share your picking ground? Or is it a secret?"

"No secret," Sarah assured him. "There's a whole field of them down where the road dead-ends. I spent at least two hours yesterday afternoon picking, and I didn't even make a dent in the crop."

He looked up, his sea green eyes quizzical. "That must have been hard work. I'm surprised you didn't sleep well. The project you mentioned must really be a bear."

Sarah's cheeks flushed slightly as she recalled her white lie. But then she quickly recovered. After all, what she'd told Matt wasn't so far from the truth. *Dream Woman* was keeping her up nights. "Yes," she agreed. "It's one of those things you have to struggle with until it comes right, and I haven't yet won the battle."

Matt took a sip of his coffee and then set down the mug. "Want to talk about it?"

Sarah shook her head quickly. No way was she going to describe that particular project to this particular man. "I'm superstitious about that sort of thing. I never talk about work in progress."

"I know what you mean," he agreed. And for a second Sarah had the impression he was going to reveal something about his own occupation, whatever that might be. But then he stopped short, an oddly guarded expression coming into his eyes. "I'm the same way," he finally said.

Sarah was suddenly curious. What did he do? she wondered. But there was no way she could question him when she'd just made her own work off limits.

Matt leaned back in his chair and cupped his hands around his mug. "Sometimes when I can't make a project come out right, the best thing for me to do is drop it for a couple of days. Why don't you try my remedy? And I have a great idea how it can be done."

"What's that?" Sarah ventured cautiously.

But he only gave her a mysterious grin. "It's something that has to be demonstrated. Let me help you clean up in here, and then I'll go home and change. When I come back to your studio this afternoon, I'll kill two birds with one stone. I'll prove there's more to my wardrobe than running shorts, and I'll show you the kind of therapy I have in mind."

Sarah was suddenly suspicious. "Oh, I don't need any help," she protested.

But Matt only grinned. Standing up, he crossed to the door. "Well, in that case, I'll see you this afternoon."

"I'm sure you have better things to do with your time—" Sarah began. Matt seemed not to hear her. Before she finished her sentence, he closed the door behind him. And a moment later he was striding briskly around the house toward the road.

She would never have invited him back this afternoon. But then she'd had no intention of asking him to breakfast. Though he seemed so pleasant and likable, he had an uncanny way of making things happen despite her wishes and, fleetingly, Sarah wondered if she was being maneuvered. But the truth was that she simply found it difficult to deny him. She liked the way he looked, the way he talked, even the sound of his rich baritone voice. She enjoyed his company—so much that for the first time in ages she began to realize just how lonely she'd been. Maybe it was time to break down some of those barriers she'd been hiding behind for the past few years. And after all, what choice did she have? Matt was coming back this afternoon. And if she turned him away when he appeared at the door, she would look like a fool.

Nevertheless, Sarah found it difficult to relax during the

29

rest of the morning. Working on something as challenging as *Dream Woman* was clearly impossible, so she brought out a few of her smaller sculptures. But try as she would to channel her thoughts into something creative, they kept inevitably returning to Matt Lyons. After a light lunch of fruit and cheese, she was just getting ready to fire several pieces in the kiln when the sound of brisk footsteps on the brick path outside alerted her to his return.

Though she was suddenly nervous and would have liked to check her appearance, she was just in the process of loading some extremely fragile green ware and couldn't leave her task.

"Come on in," she called out when she heard his voice. "I'm in the back."

A moment later Matt was peering around the corner into the alcove that housed the kiln. "That looks like a formidable piece of equipment," he commented. "Are you sure it's safe to have it in the house?"

Sarah set down the last of the objects on the kiln's shelves, propped the lid with a firebrick, and turned the switches to low. Then she inclined her head and looked at Matt. For a moment she could only gaze at him. He'd been handsome in running shorts, but in snug-fitting blue jeans and a crisp pale blue shirt, he was even more attractive.

She was glad he'd asked a question that she could answer intelligently. Otherwise, she'd just be gaping up at him.

"The kiln itself is perfectly safe," she began, "but you do have to do everything just right or you could lose the pieces being fired. These," she added, warming to the mini-lecture, "are green ware. I have to heat them up slowly and leave the lid propped for at least two hours or the gases and moisture in the clay will make them explode. And even on a second or third firing, an air bubble can do the same thing."

30

Matt grinned and held up a large, tanned hand, palm outward. "Easy," he begged lightly. "This is only my first lesson, and you don't want to short out my memory banks with too much technical information."

"Lesson?" Sarah stared at him in astonishment and then began unconsciously dusting dried clay from her jeans. "What do you mean, lesson?"

Matt snapped his fingers. "Good grief, did I forget to tell you? That's the plan for getting your mind off your problems this afternoon. You're going to give me a lesson in working with clay."

Sarah's mouth dropped open. "But . . . but I don't give lessons. I don't have time for that."

Matt looked unperturbed. "I'm one of those few under-privileged kids who never did get to make Mom an incredibly ugly clay ashtray. Probably warped my personality and stunted my psychological development. I need to make up for it."

Despite herself, Sarah found his words funny, and the corners of her mouth began to lift. Yet at the same time, somehow it was hard for her to believe that his artistic efforts, even his early ones, would be ugly.

Matt pressed his advantage. "I'm not asking for any formal instruction. Couldn't you just give me a lump of clay and let me fool around with it while you work?"

Sarah shook her head. Whatever his background, he certainly hadn't any experience with this medium.

"You can't just start fooling around with clay," she informed him. "You have to begin by wedging it properly to get the air bubbles out. And then you have to learn the principles of construction—either how to throw on a wheel or hand build."

"What do you mean by 'wedge it properly'?" Matt questioned.

Sarah moved out of the kiln alcove and across her studio to a covered crock. Lifting the lid, she reached in, scooped up several handfuls of lumpy gray material, and dumped them on a nearby table. Turning back to Matt, she gestured at the formless mass. "This is unworked stoneware clay. Right now it's too wet to shape into an ashtray. And even if you could, chances are it wouldn't fire properly because of air bubbles. Getting them out is a nuisance when you're in a hurry. But it has its compensations." As she spoke, Sarah picked up a large handful and hurled it back against the wooden table so forcefully that the legs rattled on the tile floor. Picking it up quickly, she repeated the process.

Matt's dark eyebrows shot up. "Who would have dreamed that a little thing like you could be so violent." He chuckled.

"That's how we potters maintain our serenity. We take out our aggressions on the poor, helpless clay." She hurled it against the flat surface several more times.

"Say," Matt observed. "That really looks like fun. Can I try it?"

"Sure," Sarah agreed, nodding toward the gray hunks she hadn't yet attacked. "Be my guest."

Matt picked up a large handful and hefted it in his palm. Shooting her a mischievous grin, he turned and then slammed it into the table with wood-rattling force. "That felt good," he told her. "I think I could really get to like this!"

As she continued to work her own clay, Sarah watched him from under her lashes. He really did seem to be enjoying himself. His strongly cast face had softened with amusement, and his green eyes were as intent as a kid's with a new toy.

"I think it's time to go on to the second step," she told him, placing her clay in front of her on the table. With the heels of her hands, she pressed down with all her weight until it oozed out at the ends. Then folding in the sides, she repeated the process.

Looking over at Matt, she saw him watching her actions closely. But when he began to imitate them, he didn't realize that he needed to compensate for his much greater strength. As he came down with all his weight on the clay, almost all of it squeezed out to the sides, leaving nothing under his palms. Sarah couldn't help giggling. "You've got to use a lighter touch if you don't want the whole thing to get away from you. Think of it as kneading bread."

But Matt only shook his head ruefully. "That's another experience I've missed. Maybe sometime you can teach me that, too."

The casual remark gave Sarah pause. Despite her intentions otherwise, she was undeniably giving Matt Lyons a lesson. Once again, he had managed to maneuver her into doing what he wanted. The man was downright dangerous, she told herself. And she began to suspect that behind that easy charm and handsome face there was an iron will.

But Matt quickly distracted her from her troubling speculations. Looking up, she saw him leave his own side of the table and amble around to hers.

"I seem to lack your magic touch," he remarked casually. "But maybe there's a way I can learn it. Let me feel how much pressure you're putting on that stuff."

Before she could gather her wits to protest, he had moved around in back of her and circled her waist with his arms. Leaning over her, so that she could feel his breath stirring tendrils of hair at the top of her head, he placed his large warm hands on top of hers. "Now squeeze," he whispered in her ear.

Sarah had to fight to keep her knees from buckling as she felt a hot tide of blood rushing up to her ears. Thank God he was in back of her so that he couldn't see her scarlet face. But on second thought, Sarah reasoned wildly, anything would be better than the overwhelming effect of his body pressed to hers. She could feel every muscle in his rock-hard thighs, and his wide shoulders were cradling the back of hers. As he moved slightly, the sun-darkened skin of his arm brushed her elbow, making her shiver. She knew he must have felt the tremor of sexual awareness that ran through her body.

When he spoke, his voice had deepened. "Sarah, your body fits against mine perfectly." His hands left hers so that his arms could tighten around her waist. And then she felt his lips brush softly against the top of her head.

"When I first saw you on the beach, I thought it might be like this," he murmured, his breath fanning her ear now. "I honestly wanted a pottery lesson, but I wanted to get to know you, too."

The rational part of Sarah's mind told her to break free of his unexpected embrace. But another part of her knew it wasn't unexpected at all. Ever since she'd met him she'd known what was going to happen. She'd tried to stave off the inevitable this afternoon by keeping the tone of things between them light and airy. But it hadn't worked; it couldn't have worked for long. And now the part of her that had been awaiting the next development was eager to find out what would happen next.

Slowly, Matt rotated her toward him so that she was once again wedged between his unyielding form and the table. But this time the contact was even more electrifying. For now her breasts were pressed to the hard barrier of his chest, and her hips were molded to the lower part of his body. One arm held her securely, but his other hand came up to her cheek. Sensuously, he ran a sinewy finger along the line of her jaw and then tilted her chin so that her face was tipped up to his.

He was closer to her than any man had been in a long time. And her artist's mind took in the smallest details of his features. She could see the dark tip of the lashes sur-rounding his wide-set green eyes, the strong curve of his lip, and the firm chin covered with an afternoon shadow that, like his brows, was several shades darker than his hair. And then, unexpectedly, his features broke into an impish grin.

"I forgot about the clay on my hands. I've put a streak of it on your face."

Sarah reached up to trace the same line that Matt had explored. But he quickly captured her slender fingers with his. "Don't worry. On you it looks good," he whispered. "In fact, on you everything looks good. Those hazel eyes of yours could hypnotize a man, and your eyelashes are so long they cast shadows. But it's not fair to muss you up with streaks of clay, is it?"

As he spoke, he deliberately lowered his arms to his sides and pressed her hands palm inward against his hips. But though he was no longer holding Sarah in his arms, he did not step back. To his captive, the effect was even more erotic.

It was she who was hypnotized now. Though her brain was insisting that she pull away, somehow that message was not getting through to her body. As though in a trance, she stood motionless as Matt slowly bent his head and brushed her eyelashes with his lips. The butterfly-light contact was infinitely sensual, and she shivered.

Encouraged by the response he had created, he pressed his cheek to hers, moving his head in a small circle so that the slightly rough texture of his beard tantalized her tender skin. Sarah sighed softly with pleasure, moving her own head to return the caress. For a long moment he didn't stir. And then she felt his face turn slightly so that his lips, too, could learn the feel of her cheek. As she stood transfixed, his mouth traveled softly down to the tip of her chin, where he paused to nibble sensuously at the soft flesh, his teeth a new spur to her eager awareness of this man.

Gladly she tipped her head back to give him better access. And as his mouth and teeth continued their exploration of her sensitive skin, a little involuntary gasp escaped her.

"I've been wanting to kiss you since that first morning on the beach," Matt murmured huskily, his breath fanning her now moist flesh. And then his lips were on hers. Ever so gently, with tantalizing invitation, he opened her lips, running his tongue along the silky line of her inner mouth and then teasing the barrier of her teeth, before moving boldly to the sweetness beyond. It was such an expert seduction of her senses that the female essence of Sarah could not help but respond.

Forgetting all about the clay on her own hands, she reached out and wrapped her arms around his lean waist to draw him closer. The contact broke his own self-imposed denial. With a groan, he seized her and pressed her now pliant body even tighter against the length of his hard frame. The kiss, which had been gentle, became hungry and insistent. His mouth moved on hers, testing and taking, demanding and giving. But it wasn't just the fierce passion of the kiss that made Sarah suddenly begin to realize her folly. Now that her body was molded to his, she could feel how aroused he was. And when he shifted her slightly so that his hand could cup one straining breast, Sarah stiffened. Despite, or more accurately, because of her strong response to this man, she somehow had to call a halt. But it wasn't going to be easy, now that she had allowed Matt to breach her defenses so easily.

Her hands, which had been wrapped around his waist, moved to his shoulders and began to push.

Intensely sensitive to her body, he noticed the change instantly. "What's wrong?" he whispered against her mouth.

"Please stop," she insisted. "I'm not ready for this."

She waited anxiously, half expecting that he would either get angry—or worse, redouble his efforts. But to her surprise and relief, he stepped back immediately.

"You're right," he told her huskily, putting another pace between their bodies. There was a note of regret in his voice. "I really didn't mean for things to move this fast either."

Sarah stared up at him, torn by conflicting emotions. One part of her longed to return to his arms, but not the rational, sensible part. That part was relieved and grateful that he was such a gentleman. Not many men Sarah had known in the past would have acceded to her wishes so gracefully.

"I don't want this to change things, Sarah," Matt was saying, running a hand through his thick, golden hair. "Tell me it's all right to come back tomorrow." His green eyes were so intense that she couldn't look away. It was as though he was willing her to agree.

And though she knew perfectly well that she should break things off right now, she couldn't seem to think clearly and found herself agreeing.

"Yes," she said in a low voice. "You can come back."

That was all he seemed to want for the moment. "Tomorrow afternoon," he said, before turning and striding quickly from her workshop.

Sarah was left with a disturbing mixture of feelings. What had really happened here, she asked herself, looking quizzically down at her burgundy shirt, which was now emblazoned over the right breast with powdery gray clay from Matt's hand. He had certainly left his mark on her. God, what if someone came to the door and saw her in this state, she thought, heading for the stairs. She was going to have to change.

Up in her bathroom, she could see more evidence of the damaging contact. As she gazed in the mirror at the streak of clay on her face, she remembered the feel of Matt's fingers on her skin. He might be younger that she in years but certainly not in experience. It had been ridiculously easy for him to captivate her and arouse feelings she had

37

thought were long buried. And yet, she thought, a tiny frown beginning to wrinkle her smooth forehead, he had certainly been able to turn off his own feelings quickly enough. In fact, now that she thought about it, his behavior didn't really make sense. He had felt her strong response to his lovemaking. He must have known that he could sweep aside her objections as easily as the incoming tide demolishing the defensive walls of a sand castle. But he hadn't tried. Why? she asked herself.

CHAPTER THREE

It had been a mistake to tell Matt Lyons he could come back, Sarah thought as she watched the first faint streaks of light softening the darkness outside her window. She glanced at the clock beside her bed, something she'd been doing with distressing regularity all night. It read five forty-five. She might as well get ready for her run.

There was no point in trying to avoid Matt this morning. In fact, she wanted to let him know as quickly as possible that she'd changed her mind—before this undeniable attraction between them really got out of hand.

She'd stayed up half the night manufacturing reasons why she couldn't enter into a summer romance with him. What business did a thirty-two-year-old woman have allowing a twenty-eight-year-old man to make love to her? It couldn't lead anywhere. And she simply wasn't ready for any kind of affair, much less a dead-end relationship of that type.

Even if you didn't want to consider the long-term reasons, the short-term ones were compelling enough. She had to get ready for her show in New York. It was the chance she'd been waiting for to prove herself, and Matt Lyons was a distraction she couldn't afford.

After pulling on a pair of pale blue jogging shorts and a matching T-shirt, she paused a moment to braid her luxuriant hair. The light through the window was now tinged a delicate pink, and the row of curling breakers at the edge of the beach had become a visible line of creamy white.

She stepped out onto the porch, the cool wind coming off the ocean like a tonic. And she paused for a moment to take in several lungfuls of the fresh, clean air before heading down the cut to the beach.

Twenty minutes later Sarah was in sight of the stone breakwater that usually marked the end of her run, when she caught the sound of crunching sand immediately behind her. At the light touch of a hand on her shoulder, her heart missed a beat.

Whirling, she was suddenly face to face with a grinning Matt Lyons. "You can't escape me twice," he informed her cheekily. "I was watching for you this morning."

For a moment she could only stare at him in blank surprise while she struggled to catch her breath. And then she found her voice.

"Watching for me?"

"Yes," he replied with a wicked light in his emerald eyes. "I was afraid you might get away from me again. So I kept an eye out."

"Was sneaking up on me like that part of your detective act?" she questioned dryly, folding her arms protectively across her chest. Now that she wasn't running anymore, the ocean breeze had begun to chill her flushed skin.

"Well, I did call out to you several times. But I guess you didn't hear," he defended.

Sarah blinked and looked quickly down at the toes of her running shoes. The truth was that while her feet had been pounding rhythmically against the sand, her thoughts had been directed so firmly inward that she probably wouldn't have heard a bomb go off. She had been thinking about what she was going to say to him. But she certainly didn't intend to tell him that. Instead of answering, she turned and began to walk back toward her house.

Matt fell in beside her, and for a few hundred paces they

made their way along the beach with only the rushing sound of the waves filling the silence between them.

"You look like you're a million miles away. Penny for your thoughts," he finally ventured.

Sarah knew she could no longer postpone the little speech she'd been preparing since last night. "Listen, Matt," she began. "About this afternoon. I think it would be better if you didn't come for any more lessons."

There was another long silence while the tall, blond man took in her words. "Why, Sarah?" he finally asked quietly.

She swallowed. This was going to be even harder than she'd anticipated. "Well, I have this show to get ready for. It's really important to me, and I haven't got time to let anything interfere."

Even to her own ears, the excuse that had sounded so compelling in the middle of the night now seemed lame. After all, not even the most dedicated artist could spend twenty-four hours a day being creative. And in a moment it became clear that Matt had no intention of accepting the explanation. Stopping, he put his hand on her shoulder so that she, too, was forced to halt. "Be honest with me, Sarah; that's just a cop-out. That isn't what you really mean, is it?"

Sarah took a deep breath. "All right. No, it isn't," she finally admitted in a small voice.

"Then what's this all about?" he persisted.

"We're both adults, and you know perfectly well what it's all about," she shot back. "Don't try to tell me you don't have more in mind than pottery lessons . . ."

Sarah was about to complete her sentence when she noticed the change of expression on Matt's striking features. Underneath his tan he'd gone pale, and she wondered for a split second at his strong reaction. But she was too caught up in the flow of her own thoughts to stop now. "Look, there's no denying that we're attracted to each other. But I'm older than you are, and I'm not interested in a summer romance that can't go anywhere."

The relief that flooded his face was startling. "So that's it." Maddeningly, he looked amused now. "My God, Sarah. If you've got any years on me, you sure don't look it. How old are you, anyway?"

"I was thirty-two last April," she informed him very seriously.

In response, he broke into loud laughter. "Practically a senior citizen."

Sarah found her face reddening with irritation and embarrassment. "Just what's so damn funny?" she demanded.

Matt struggled to contain his amusement. "Four years and you're making it sound like you're Mae West and I'm a Cub Scout. Come on, Sarah, you can do better than that. What's really bothering you?"

Somehow his irreverent reaction was like the jab of a spur to a skittish horse. "I just can't handle this sort of thing right now," she blurted before turning deliberately away and fixing her gaze on the now gray-blue horizon.

Matt stood directly behind her, looking down at the top of her dark head. "Somehow you're making me feel like an unprepared understudy who's been pushed onto the stage in the third act. What's happened to make you feel this way?"

Sarah shivered, but she didn't respond.

"Going to force me to do all the talking?" he questioned, his deep voice edged only slightly with self-deprecating humor. "Then I'll just have to plunge ahead until I find the answer to this riddle by myself. But maybe it's not so difficult, after all. I assume you didn't spend your first thirty-two years in a cloister, Sarah. So there must have been some other men in your life. Did one of them hurt you so badly that you're afraid to take a chance on another relationship? Is that why you're turning me off?"

Sarah waited tensely for what might come next. And then, unexpectedly, Matt's left hand shot out and seized hers. "No ring."

"But there used to be one there," Sarah whispered. "I divorced him four years ago."

There was a brief period of silence while Matt absorbed that bit of information. "I suppose you think you've answered my question," he finally observed. "But four years is a long time."

An ironic smile began to curve Sarah's mouth. "You just got done telling me that four years is nothing," she pointed out.

Matt turned her toward him once more, so that she could see the frustration in his face. "All right, so I painted myself into a corner," he admitted wryly. "But don't pretend you don't know what I mean. Four years doesn't mean anything between the two of us. But it's a long time to spend brooding over a guy who couldn't be worth much—not if he was fool enough to let you go, anyway."

Sarah sighed. "I meant what I said, Matt. I really can't handle something like this now. And you're not going to talk me out of it."

As soon as the words were out of her mouth, Sarah realized she'd made a mistake. Matt's expression shifted from serious to mischievous. "Ah, but I didn't exactly have talking in mind," he informed her.

With that, Sarah found his hands tightening on her shoulders, and then one of them slipped sensually down the line of her back to her waist and drew her tightly against his body.

The steady wind off the ocean and her confused emotions during the conversation had chilled her. But the sudden contact with Matt's flesh made her go warm all over. She was vividly aware of his bare, hair-textured legs

43

pressed to her smooth ones. That, combined with the gentle but uncompromising pressure of his arms around her back and his broad chest against her breasts, was excruciatingly sensual. Despite all her doubts, Sarah found herself giving in to it.

But Matt had only just begun his persuasive efforts. His head lowered so that he could nuzzle the delicate shell of her ear. "Sarah," he whispered, "I know you've been having a rough time lately, but you have to give us a chance."

She couldn't answer. She was too overwhelmed by his nearness and the turmoil of her own feelings. And Matt wasn't giving her a chance to clear her mind. Seductively, his lips slid down from her ear to her throat while at the same time his hands moved to her hips to press her even tighter against his hard frame. "I won't hurry or pressure you. Let's just see where things go. Let me spend time with you. I'll stay away from your studio if you want, but let me take you out."

Sarah stirred restlessly, still torn between reason and desire. But Matt stilled her by lifting his head and brushing his lips against hers. The first touch was feather light. And yet it made her move instinctively closer to him. With that, his mouth molded itself to hers. His lips teased hers open so that his tongue could brush insistently against the line of her teeth, quickly dispatching yet another obstacle to his sensual invasion.

As his tongue took hot possession of her mouth she felt her body shudder with helpless longing. She should send him away now, but she couldn't find the strength for that. Standing here, folded in his arms, felt so right. And there was no way she could not welcome his kiss. Sensing her acquiescence, he deepened his exploration, seeking out and finding what gave her the most pleasure. It was no longer within her power to remain passive. The tip of her own tongue stole forward to find his, wantonly increasing the erotic stimulation. The abandoned gesture told him all he needed to know. And yet denying himself this sweet fulfillment was difficult beyond belief.

After all too short a moment, he finally forced himself to draw back slightly.

"Ah, Sarah," he murmured, "if I don't quit now, I won't be able to. . . . Have dinner with me tonight," he murmured huskily. "I want to see you, but I won't push you into anything you're not ready for."

Despite all her doubts, Sarah found herself nodding. "All right," she agreed. Even though she had tried to persuade herself otherwise, she did want to go on seeing this man.

Strangely, once Sarah had accepted Matt's invitation, she felt an overwhelming sense of relief. He had released her from his embrace at once and, though there was a lingering current of sensuality between them, their walk back along the beach was as lighthearted as their first meeting. This time, instead of accompanying her home, he left her on the beach.

"I have things to do today, too," he told her. "But I'll come by for you at six o'clock. Over cocktails you can report on all the progress you've made without me around messing up your studio."

Fleetingly Sarah wondered what *things* Matt had to do. Wasn't he supposed to be on vacation? But thoughts of her own work waiting in the studio quickly brushed any other considerations aside.

Somehow Matt's admonitions about making progress were like a magic charm. After he left her, Sarah's day seemed to fly past. She finished several of the smaller pieces she'd put aside as particularly difficult. And when she uncovered *Dream Woman,* she found herself looking at the sculpture with new eyes. Suddenly she felt more confident about achieving what she wanted and tackled the work with renewed zest.

But though she was enjoying her creative efforts more than she had in days, she wasn't so unaware of the outside world that she lost track of time. And, in fact, by five o'clock she found her mind wandering to what she would wear. After covering her work and storing the leftover clay in a crock, Sarah went upstairs to bathe and take stock of her closet.

Though she had an elegant wardrobe, she hadn't worn much other than T-shirts and jeans since her last trip to New York early that spring. What should she put on this evening? she wondered, realizing suddenly that Matt hadn't said where they were going. Since most of the restaurants in the area were casual, she finally selected a sun dress in a raspberry shade that brought out the glow of her skin and emphasized the golden lights in her hazel eyes. On impulse, she swept her thick dark hair into a Victorian roll, leaving loose tendrils to curl softly around her ears and forehead. A light coat of pink lip gloss, a dusting of ash green eye shadow, and a dab of lemony cologne completed her toilette.

Her smoothly tanned legs required no stockings. She was just slipping into a pair of strappy white sandals when she heard the sound of a car pulling up the drive, followed by a firm knock on the front door.

Giving herself one last approving glance in the cheval mirror that had stood in her room since she was a child, Sarah went downstairs and opened the door to Matt.

The sight of him almost took her breath away. He had been more than attractive in jogging shorts and jeans, but in an expensively cut buff sport coat and hip-hugging tan slacks he was startling. His burnished hair was brushed smoothly back from his forehead, and his green eyes were a sparkling contrast to the deep tan of his chiseled features.

But apparently his reaction to her own transformation was every bit as strong. "Well, I see I've already got my

46

reward," he murmured, his gaze taking her in possessively. "What happened to your braids? Are you sure you're the same ragamuffin I met on the beach this morning? She was cute. But you're absolutely beautiful."

Sarah blushed. She'd heard plenty of compliments from men before. But somehow Matt's words affected her much more strongly. To disguise her reaction, she returned the accolade lightly. "You look pretty sharp yourself. I hope I'm not going to have to fight off all the women in the restaurant this evening."

Matt laughed. "I certainly hope not. Anyway, the place I'm taking you to is dimly lit, so it ought to be pretty safe," he added lightheartedly. "It's a little restaurant down in Woods Hole overlooking the harbor. I picked it because it's quiet and the food is excellent."

Sarah knew the one he had described. It was a longtime favorite—a rustic wharf building that had been converted into a charming dining room with stained glass windows, hatch-cover tables, and wooden decks overlooking the water.

Matt had reserved a windowside table where they could see the many sailboats anchored in the sheltered harbor.

"I'm glad you found this place," Sarah enthused as they sipped their gin and tonics. "I can't wait to go down and pick my lobster out of the tank."

For a moment there was a disconcerted expression on Matt's face, and then he took a quick gulp of his drink and turned his attention back to the menu.

"I think I'll stick with the crab-stuffed flounder," he observed from behind his large glossy menu.

"But lobster's the specialty here. And it's really delicious," Sarah insisted.

Matt closed his menu and shook his head stubbornly. "I prefer not to see my dinner swimming around just before I eat it."

Sarah cocked her head quizzically. "Are you saying that you're squeamish?" she questioned.

Her dinner companion grinned sheepishly. "I can't look one of those little red guys in the eye knowing I'm sealing his fate."

"But you're having crab with your flounder," Sarah pointed out. "What's the difference?"

"The difference is that someone in the kitchen took care of the necessary preliminaries. I don't have to take moral responsibility for it. All I have to do is eat it."

Sarah laughed out loud. "I've been wondering what you do for a living. I guess I can cross 'chef' off my list."

Matt took a careful sip of his drink and then set it down on the table. "You're right, I'm not a chef. Right now I'm in the middle of a big project that's been giving me a lot of sleepless nights. That's one of the reasons I came up here to Cape Cod—so I could turn it over in my mind. But I'm like you, Sarah. I don't want to talk about my work when it hasn't jelled for me yet. Let's just relax and enjoy dinner together, shall we?"

Sarah nodded. He was referring to the way she'd been so quick to turn him off *Dream Woman* the other day. And he was right, she thought. He was entitled to his privacy. Still, she couldn't help being curious. Most men wanted to talk about their jobs. Why was Matt so reticent?

As if to distract her thoughts, he quickly turned the conversation to other topics. And as they sipped their drinks and ate their dinner, she found they had a surprising number of interests and opinions in common. They both liked classical music, admired the French Impressionists, enjoyed body surfing in the summer and skiing in the winter, and hated seeing the Cape overdeveloped and overrun by too many tourists.

The conversation that had been flowing so smoothly, however, came to a halt when Matt brought up the subject of family.

"How did you get into skiing?" he asked innocently. "Was yours the kind of family that went off on ski trips together?"

Sarah's relaxed smile tightened. "No, I learned at a Swiss boarding school," she told him matter-of-factly, hoping he wouldn't pursue the topic.

Matt's eyebrows lifted. "Pretty classy. You live in a nice house, but I wouldn't have pegged you for an heiress. Why did your family send you abroad?"

Sarah was becoming uncomfortable. She'd spent two years in Switzerland during a time when her father was very busy in Hollywood and her mother was having trouble coping with a teenage daughter alone. But she felt that kind of private information was just that—private. "Oh, just the usual reasons," she finally told him. "But let's talk about something else."

Though he gave her an appraising look, Matt made no objection. And once again he was able to steer the conversation onto more amiable ground.

However, when they were alone in his silver sports car, Sarah found herself growing tense. Would Matt kiss her again tonight, and how would she react? she wondered. Her stomach tightened with anticipation, and a little shiver ran up her spine. But, to her surprise, and somewhat to her chagrin, when Matt saw her to the door, he only brushed the top of her forehead with his lips before saying good night and turning to leave.

In fact, over the next few days, he took pains to make sure the relationship was undemanding.

The effect on Sarah was not what she would have expected. Instead of feeling relieved she grew strangely restless. This was what she had told him she wanted, but was it really? They had several more companionable dinners that week. And Sarah found herself waiting expectantly for him to take her in his arms each time they arrived at her door. Instead, he departed abruptly.

It was only on what she thought of as their fourth "date" that he lingered in front of her house.

"The night's so fine, it's a shame to waste it," he declared. "How about coming down to the beach and stargazing with me?"

Sarah looked up at the night sky. It was like a dome of velvet studded with twinkling jewels, set off by the dim radiance of the moon in its third quarter.

"You're right," she agreed, waiting as Matt stopped to take a blanket from the car. Side by side they walked down the cut to a stretch of beach sheltered by the dunes, and Matt spread the blanket and sat down. A week ago, the intimacy of the quiet setting might have worried her. But his almost diffident behavior over the past few days had changed her expectations. Although she couldn't quite admit it, now it was she who wanted to make something happen between them. She just wasn't sure exactly what.

"Look at those stars," Matt exclaimed, leaning back so that he could look up at the resplendent night sky. "In New York, you can't see half as many."

Sarah chuckled. "And in LA, you can't see any of them. And then, realizing it was the kind of statement that might bring forth one of Matt's unwelcome questions, she tensed.

But tonight he chose to probe no further. The two of them seemed to be establishing a relationship that existed only in the here and now. She didn't want to talk about her past, and he didn't want to talk about his work. And for the moment, that suited her perfectly.

"I feel as though I can almost touch those stars," he remarked, lying back so that he had a full view of the heavens. Sarah nestled down beside him. The night was a warm one, and he had taken off his sports coat before driving home. Sarah felt a prickle of sensation where the hair of his bare arm brushed against hers. But she didn't move away. She wanted the contact. In fact, if she were

50

honest she would admit that she had been craving his closeness all week.

With studied casualness, she rubbed her arm against his, enjoying the little shiver the further intimacy created. But Matt didn't move, seeming unaware of her reaction.

His lack of response was maddening and frustrating. Why was he acting so differently? she wondered. Unable to endure his indifference, Sarah nuzzled her face against his shoulder—all at once aware of the very male scent of this man lying next to her under the stars. Suddenly, it was almost impossible for Sarah to abide by the rules that she herself had set for their relationship. Without really thinking about what she was doing, she reached down almost as though the motion were random and brushed her hand against the outside of his thigh.

This time, his response was instantaneous. "Sarah, don't," he whispered, meshing his fingers with hers so that he could pull her hand away.

So that was it, she realized. Things had changed between them. He didn't want her anymore, and she was simply making a fool of herself. She turned her head away and quickly began to rise to her feet.

But when she started to get up, Matt's hand shot out to circle her wrist. "Don't go."

"Why not?" she challenged. "It's obvious that—"

"Nothing's obvious," he corrected, his eyes searching her face with an odd mixture of longing and regret. God, she was beautiful in the moonlight, he thought, drinking in the way the dim radiance silvered her delicate features. She didn't know how much he longed to run his fingers along the soft curve of her cheek and down the proud length of her ivory throat. And he wanted more than that. He wanted to pull her into his arms and fit her body to his. The careful restraint he'd imposed upon himself this last week had been torture. But he'd forced himself to pull back. It was only fair to Sarah. Yet, tonight he hadn't been able to simply leave her off at the door. He'd wanted to prolong the evening. And so he'd suggested coming down here to the beach. Now he knew that had been a mistake.

He'd wanted Sarah physically from the moment he'd first set eyes on her. But he'd wanted information, too. At first he'd tried to tell himself that there need be no conflict between the two purposes. What did one have to do with the other, after all? But now that he'd gotten to know Sarah, she'd become more than just a desirable body. She was a woman with a great deal of sensitivity. He hadn't known about the damage her divorce had done when he'd first met her. But he'd known a lot about her father. Had she discovered the old man's relationship with Marjorie Winter? If so, she was probably hurt and shocked that her mother hadn't been the only important woman in his life. And that might be part of her problem.

He wanted to reach out and help heal her wounds— whatever they might be. But would she let him if she knew why he had contrived to meet her in the first place. The thought made his stomach knot. That was why he'd been holding off these last few days, even though he burned for her. But just now, her seemingly casual gesture had let him know for the first time that the strong attraction might be mutual and that she might be feeling the same needs he'd been wrestling with all week. The realization was more than he could handle, and all at once the desire that had been simmering within him for days burst its bounds.

With the hand that still held her wrist captive, Matt pulled Sarah back down beside him on the blanket. And then, before the look of surprise had time to register on her delicate features, he was covering her body with his. Unable to hold back the urgency he felt, his mouth descended unhesitatingly to hers in a kiss that was as much a demand as a promise.

And yet, deep within him, there was a part that still held

back, waiting for her response. Her touch had set things in motion, but if she withdrew from him once again, he would understand.

But there was no hesitancy in Sarah now. There was no way she could pull away from him tonight. Matt Lyons had unlocked a door inside her that she had held firmly shut until they had met that morning on the beach. Eagerly she opened to him, welcoming the exploration of his lips and tongue. She was beyond thought, beyond reason as her arms wound around his shoulder, pulling him even closer against her. A week of being with him and not touching or holding or caressing had done its work on her, too. And now the fire coursing through her veins was out of control.

Her ardent response was a provocation to his own need. And now he could not get enough of her. His lips left hers to feather provocative little kisses across her cheeks and along the line of her jaw, while his hands traveled up and down her sides, feeling with pleasure the firm flesh over her ribs and the rounded swell of her hips.

Leaning back slightly, he looked down into the depths of her hazel eyes, seeing his own burning passion mirrored there. And then, he bent to kiss the pulse point at the base of her throat.

Sarah stirred against him, wanting more, wanting the same thing he did. And when he sought her breasts through the thin material of her sun dress, she found that she could hardly breathe.

His own ragged breath caught in his throat as he felt her nipples harden beneath his fingers. And then his hands went to her shoulders. She knew at once what he would do next. Shivering in anticipation, she felt him slide the straps of her dress off her shoulders so that he could draw the bodice down and away from her upper body.

For a moment he paused to drink in her beauty. And then he bent to bury his face in the valley between her creamy breasts, turning his head first one way and then the other to revel in their softness against his face.

The effect on Sarah was electrifying. With a little sigh of joy she reached down to caress the back of his head, twining her fingers in the thick golden hair as she had wanted to do for so long.

When his lips found one throbbing nipple and took it into his mouth, her body arched upward against his long, lean frame.

She was his captive now, bound to him by a web of passion that she had barely understood until a few moments ago. And yet, if she were his captive, so was he hers.

"God, I've been wanting this for so long," he whispered huskily, his mouth against her soft flesh.

"Yes."

There were many things she had wanted from this man. And although she had not dared before to form most of her desires into conscious thoughts, she was suddenly no longer able to deny herself—to maintain the veneer of composure she had been so careful to present. With impatient fingers, she undid the buttons of his shirt, slipping her hands inside at last so that she could stroke the broad, muscled span of his chest.

"God, Sarah, I've been wanting that, too," he murmured, his own hands moving upward to caress her cheeks, her lips, her hair.

"Yes," she answered again, delighting in the glory of touching and being touched.

And yet it was hardly enough. There was more that they each wanted, infinitely much more. With sudden urgency, Matt pulled Sarah into his arm, twining his legs with hers so that the lower part of her body was brought tightly up against his own. At once she was burningly aware of his need. And the intimate contact was a vivid enticement to her own rising passion.

Moaning deep in her throat, she began to sway her hips

against his in unspoken invitation, bringing forth an answering growl of passion from deep in Matt's throat.

Moving back slightly so that he could find the zipper of her sun dress, he began to remove the barrier to their intimacy. And as he slowly drew the brightly printed fabric down over her hips, his thumbs found the edge of her lacy panties so he could remove these, too, at the same time. His hands were a tender caress as he shed the last of her clothing. And then he began working his way up her body again, trailing stinging little kisses along the silken skin of her legs. At the same time, he ran his hand sensually up the insides of first one thigh and then the other, moving closer, ever closer to the molten core of her desire. The teasing touch was almost more than Sarah could bear. And without realizing what she was doing, she reached down to clasp his hand and press it upward to that part of her which most longed for his attentions.

"Ah, Sarah," she heard him gasp, for he had wanted this intimacy as much as she. With gentle sureness, he began to stroke and caress her, seeking, testing, finding the secrets of her desire. She felt her whole body quiver under the magic of his knowing touch. And now it was his name that came unbidden to her lips. "Matt, please," she choked out, all but inarticulate from the sweet torture his fingers were inflicting.

But he knew what it was she wanted. For him, too, the urgency of desire was now almost more than he could bear. It took him only a moment to remove his own clothes. And then he was pulling Sarah into his arms and covering her soft body with the hard length of his own. He ached now to plunge into her, to swiftly complete that most intimate of embraces. And yet he knew as surely as if she had told him that he was the first to make love to her in a long, long time.

And so, with all the willpower he possessed, he forced himself to go slowly and cautiously, watching her face so he would know if he were causing her pain. His reward was the look of pure rapture that spread across her features as he finally made her completely his own.

He felt her arms go around his shoulders, then kneading and stroking as she pulled him closer, the extent of her craving for fulfillment apparent in her imploring touch.

"Oh, yes, Sarah," he whispered, "ohhh, yes," beginning at last to move inside her. He marveled at how perfect this felt, how right, as thought it were inevitable from the beginning of time that their bodies would one day come together in this way.

For Sarah there were no thoughts now, only the exquisite sensations he was creating. There were no words on her lips, only incoherent little moans of ecstasy. Her own hips surged forward fiercely to meet his every stroke as he increased the rhythm of their passion, pushing them up and upward to the very limits of pleasure. It was as though her body had caught fire from his. And when the ultimate explosion came, it was like a thousand shooting stars blazing across the dome of the heavens above them.

Yet, though shooting stars flare heavenward, making glorious displays across the velvety sky, they inevitably spend their power and fall to earth. And so it was for Sarah. No sooner had her passion flared to fulfillment and drained her, than her mind returned to the sanity Matt's lovemaking had banished. Dazedly, she looked up at the man who crushed her beneath his body. She was there because she wanted to be. But what had she done? she asked herself, turning her head away from him. What in the world had she done?

spite what he said, age was still a problem in her mind. A sexual relationship with him had no place to go, she told herself. Right now she might not look any older than he, but would that always be true? And then there was the question of children. At twenty-eight, Matt was probably not thinking in those terms. Men were often not ready to settle down and have families until they were in their mid-thirties. But if she were ever to get pregnant, it would have to be in the next few years. The four years he made so light of could generate a thousand difficulties, some of which she was probably not even able to foresee.

But he was right, it wasn't what was really eating at her now. Her marriage had left her with a strong feeling of vulnerability. Her art had been her salvation. It had been something on which she could focus, something to which she could devote her life. If anything, her father's affair with Marjorie Winter had reinforced her mistrust of male-female relationships. She was afraid to let herself be this closely involved with a man. And the strong response Matt seemed to be able to elicit from her so easily made her even more fearful. What if she gave her trust to him, allowed herself to be vulnerable to him, and he hurt her the way Brad had? At this critical point in her life, when so much depended on her ability to concentrate on her work, she didn't think she could go through another experience like that.

Matt's eyes still questioned hers. Could she really trust him? she wondered. And then she remembered their lovemaking. Matt had inspired an overpowering need in her and then met it with his own. Brad had never made her lose herself like that. In fact, she hadn't known lovemaking could be so fiery and so satisfying. Surely that meant what was between them shouldn't be carelessly tossed aside. Maybe it was worth taking a chance and giving him her trust as she had already given him her body a few minutes ago.

"Matt," she repeated, "you're right. And you're wrong, too. Those four years do worry me, but there are things that worry me more. There's a lot I've never explained about myself, and I can't tell you about it now. But I've had some bad experiences in the past few years. Before I left Brad, I walked in on him in bed with another woman. You don't know what that did to my self-confidence."

Matt's features hardened. "I'd like to get my hands on that bastard," he began. "I understand now that he's scarred you badly. And I can see those wounds haven't healed. But, Sarah, don't make me pay for that. I know what we can have together is special. Give it a chance. Maybe we both got carried away tonight. I should have realized that you weren't ready for this. But I couldn't help myself any more than you could."

Sarah gazed up at his strongly cast face, touched with the silver of the moonlight. The sight of him made her heart melt. And she found herself reaching out with trembling fingers to brush his lean cheek, feeling the sandpapery texture of his beard.

Gently he captured her hand and stilled it in his. "Promise you won't stop seeing me, Sarah," he whispered. "And I'll promise that when we make love again, it will only be when you really want it."

She was still afraid. And yet how could she refuse what he was offering? Lowering her lashes, she whispered, "I don't know what to say, Matt."

"Then say yes," he urged, his warm hands stroking down the silken length of her naked back. The sensation sent delicious shivers up her spine. And it was only with the greatest self-control that she kept her body from arching sensuously against his once again.

"How can I think when you're doing this to me?" she protested.

He chuckled as his hand ran softly down the inner

length of her thigh. "That's the idea. And I won't stop until you give me an answer."

"Until I give you the answer you want to hear," she corrected, feeling her blood race as his fingers stroked a delicate pattern on the yielding flesh of her buttock. She had to stop him, or explode. And the only way seemed to be to give him what he wanted now.

"Yes," she breathed, her face turned in against his shoulder. At once the maddening stroking stopped, and his arms moved up to encircle her waist. "You won't regret this, Sarah—I promise you."

Though she'd had her doubts, during the next few days Matt proved himself to be a man of his word. It had been hard for her to believe that after their lovemaking, he could go back to treating her with the casual camaraderie he'd shown earlier. But, to her surprise, that was exactly what happened. When he met her for their morning run on the beach, he joked and pulled her braid and made her laugh. And when she agreed to accompany him to a nearby country fair, they rode the Ferris wheel and merry-go-round and stuffed themselves with cotton candy like children.

"I haven't done this sort of thing since I was twelve years old," he told her with a delighted grin.

Sarah felt her own expression sober. "I never did this sort of thing," she confessed. "My mother would have considered this a frivolous waste of time, and my father was too busy with his work."

Matt regarded her thoughtfully. "What kind of a deprived childhood did you have, anyway?"

"I never realized it was deprived—till later," she returned. "But I don't want to talk about that now. Let's try The Whip next." She pointed to the spinning circle of garishly painted cars just visible on the other side of the fairgrounds.

But before she could head in that direction, Matt placed

a firm hand on her shoulder. "Every time I mention your family, you clam up. Until you're willing to tell me that sort of thing, we're never going to get past whatever's troubling you."

Sarah's gaze slid away from his. "Matt, I just want to have a good time with you this afternoon. Let's not get too heavy."

Matt shrugged. "All right, we'll have it your way," he agreed, pulling her close and giving her shoulder a squeeze. That set the tone for the rest of the afternoon.

And yet, after Matt had dropped her off and Sarah was once again alone in her studio, she wondered if he wasn't right. Maybe she did have to trust him and open up with him more if she was going to lay the foundation for a solid relationship.

It was the next day, while they were driving along a graveled lane that roughly paralleled the coast, that she had the opportunity to put her new resolve into practice. "Stop over there," she suggested with a smile, pointing to a stand of wind-gnarled pines that screened the coastline from the road.

Obediently, Matt maneuvered his low-slung sports car off onto the grass and then turned toward her expectantly. The convertible top of the car was down. And the wind had blown some fair locks of his thick hair across his forehead. Playfully, she reached up to push them back.

"Maybe I'll have to grow it long enough for a pigtail like yours," Matt observed.

"That was your idea, not mine," she retorted easily, opening the door and stepping out onto the sandy soil. "This used to be one of my favorite places to hide out when I was a kid and I wanted to show it to you."

He looked around curiously at the rather unassuming landscape. "I don't see . . ." he began.

Sarah grinned. "That's the beauty of this place. You can't tell from the road that there's anything here to see.

But just wait." Impulsively grabbing his hand, she tugged him toward an overgrown path just barely visible on the other side of an elderberry bush.

Good-naturedly, Matt allowed himself to be led through the woods and down a rocky slope to a small, beautiful inlet screened on all sides by the thick stand of trees. Dropping his hand, Sarah gestured expansively at the scenic spot. "My private pool," she proclaimed. "I found this one day when I was looking for wild flowers to dry. It turned into my special place. When I was a teenager I used to come here and brood. And even now, when I need to be by myself to think, I sometimes pack a lunch and spend the afternoon here."

Matt put his hands on his narrow, blue-jean-clad hips and looked around appreciatively at the small pool of azure water framed by the heavy curtain of deep green foliage. And then his gaze returned to Sarah. For a few seconds his expression was thoughtful. Then a slow smile spread across his features. "Do you ever skinny-dip when you're here alone?" he asked.

To her annoyance, Sarah felt herself blush. As a matter of fact, she had. But that was a secret she hadn't planned on sharing with Matt.

Her self-conscious expression made him throw back his head and laugh. "I can see that you did. And why not, it's certainly the perfect spot for it," he pointed out, reaching down to pull off the gray knit shirt he was wearing.

"What . . . what are you doing?" Sarah gasped, taking in the tanned muscularity of his now naked upper body.

"I think you have the right idea. This place was made for skinny-dipping." He turned away from her and she heard the sound of a zipper. Sarah's eyes widened as she saw his hands go to the waistband of his jeans and begin to push them down. In the next instant the darkly tanned skin of his lower back gave way to the pale firmness of masculine buttocks.

Blushing even more furiously, Sarah hurriedly averted her eyes and turned back toward the trees. "Matt, for heaven's sake! What if someone should see?"

The only answer to her question was the barely detectable sound of retreating footsteps on the rocky ground, followed by a splash.

Sarah whirled around again only to see Matt's head and flashing grin emerge above the blue surface of the water. Pushing water-darkened strands of hair out of his eyes, he called out to her. "Come on in, the water's fine!"

"Are you crazy? Didn't you hear what I said? What if someone should see?"

But Matt was nonchalant. "I'm not ashamed of my body and neither should you be. Take off your clothes and come on in," he urged again. Rolling over on his stomach, he stretched his powerful arms over his head, submerged his face, and began a rhythmic flutter kick that quickly took him to the center of the quiet cove. Sarah watched his long, elegantly muscled form as it shot through the crystal water. He was obviously a good swimmer, and she could picture him racing on a team in high school or college. Had he done that? she wondered, suddenly curious about his past. As if he knew she were watching, Matt lifted his head and took a breath of air. Then he executed a sudden hairpin flip so that his well-shaped calves and feet pointed skyward before disappearing below the water's surface.

Sarah waited for him to reemerge. But as the long seconds crawled by and the water's smooth patina remained unruffled, she began to grow anxious. What had happened? Could he have hit his head on a rock? Unconsciously, she began to move closer to the water's edge.

"Matt?" she called out uncertainly, starting to kick off her sandals. When there was no answer, her voice took on a terror-sharpened edge. "Matt!" Hastily, her fingers fumbled with the closure on her waistband. As her skirt slid down around her ankles, there was a loud whoosh, and Matt's head and shoulders shot up through the water, creating a small geyser of spray.

Shaking the droplets out of his eyes, he took in her half-undressed state. "Damn! I came up too soon," he chortled.

Sarah shot him a murderous glare. "You, you devil! What were you doing under there all this time? I thought you might be drowning or something."

"Just seeing if I could still swim a hundred yards under water. It didn't occur to me that you'd be concerned enough to come to my rescue. But now that you're half-undressed, why don't you come on in? If you're shy, I'll look the other way."

Sarah hesitated. The sun was hot and the water certainly did look inviting—even more so now that Matt was smiling up at her like Neptune tempting her to his kingdom. She supposed it really was silly to put on such a prudish act, when in fact they *had* been lovers. He had explored her body—and not just with his eyes. His hands and lips had discovered her most intimate feminine secrets. And yet, somehow she couldn't quite bring herself to boldly undress before him in broad daylight.

Seeing the conflict of expressions on her face and reading her emotions accurately, Matt relented. "All right, my shy little naiad, I'll turn around and you can preserve your modesty."

As good as his word, he swiveled in the water so that all she could see was his gleaming shoulders and the smooth contours of his damp head. Feeling rather foolish, she quickly unbuttoned her blouse and unhooked her bra. As she began to slide her lacy panties down her hips, Matt flicked up a miniature plume of water with his thumb and forefinger, and she squeaked.

"Just seeing how ready you are," he teased. "But don't worry. I'm not going to turn around."

"You'd better not," she warned, lowering herself quickly into the cool water. It slid up over her heated body like a silken hand. But to her dismay, instead of completely hiding the front of her body, it only brushed the pink tips of her jutting breasts.

As Matt turned toward her, his green eyes fastened on the pearly white globes. Quickly she brought up her hands to shield herself from his burning gaze. But not before he had taken in the inviting curves of her upper body.

"You don't need to hide yourself from me, Sarah," he said quietly. "You're beautiful. Don't you know that?"

But before she could answer, he turned and struck out with vigorous strokes toward the opposite side of the cove. It was as though, having finally coaxed her into the water, her naked presence was too disturbing and he needed to escape.

Sarah watched him swim away with painfully mixed emotions. Part of her wished he would pull her into his arms and crush her body against the lean firmness of his. Seeing his magnificent body had made her remember with shattering clarity just how thrilling it had been to meld herself with him. But part of her was grateful for his restraint. She looked around at the idyllic scene. This secluded cove was as tempting as paradise must have been to the first lovers, yet Matt was leashing the sensual side of his nature and allowing her the time and the space she needed.

Sarah moved deeper into the water until her feet no longer touched bottom and began a leisurely sidestroke away from him. He seemed content to let her swim on her own. But she still felt his presence on the other side of the cove as though an invisible bond tethered them to one another.

A while later, she began to feel a bit cold. How was she going to get out? she wondered, glancing in Matt's direction.

He waved. "Had enough?"

"Yes," Sarah admitted. "But are you going to be a gentleman and turn your back so that I can get out?"

He began to swim in her direction. "I'm nothing if not gentlemanly," he told her wryly. "In fact, I'll even let you dry yourself off with my shirt—unless you'd rather just stretch out in the sun, that is."

"I think I'll accept the offer of the shirt," Sarah responded, backing away slightly in the water. Matt was close enough now so that she could glimpse the powerful outlines of his lower body in the water. He must be seeing her, too, though his expression gave no sign.

Suddenly, against her will, an image of Matt taking her into his arms in this secluded pool and making the kind of passionate, searing love that had lifted her to never-before-experienced heights of ecstasy on the beach began to play through her mind with devastating effect. Though she had told herself she was glad Matt was showing such self-control, for a treacherous moment she couldn't help regretting his command over himself. Her own body was betraying her now. And she could feel a heated tightness beginning to build inside her. Embarrassed by her weakness, she turned away.

"You promised not to look," she reminded him, striking out for the shore. Without waiting for his reply she hoisted herself out of the water, conscious of how her naked body must look with droplets of water still clinging to her pink flesh and glistening like diamonds in the sun. Was Matt watching? she wondered. Though she'd ordered him not to, he hadn't actually agreed. Despite herself, she moved toward the heap of clothes with slow, almost languorously seductive movements. Bending down gracefully to lift his soft knit shirt, she began to dab at the damp skin of her arms, half-hoping that Matt was watching and that he would come out of the water and join her—perhaps even take her in his arms. But when she looked up from

67

under her lashes, he was floating quietly on his back, his arms behind his head while he gazed peacefully up at the sky.

An irrational dart of annoyance stabbed at her, and she threw down his shirt. Stepping over it, she grabbed at her clothes and began to drag them on, oblivious to the wetness of her skin.

She tried to tell herself that she was reacting to her own ambiguous feelings. But it was more than that. Illogical as it might seem, she was annoyed by Matt's self-control as well. How could she know where she stood with him? At one moment he was pursuing her like an Indian tracking a doe. At the next he was treating her with the casual friendliness of a brother for a favorite sister. What exactly were his feelings toward her? she asked herself.

She had been fully dressed for several minutes when Matt called out, "Ready?"

"Yes," she muttered.

Matt began to stroke easily toward her. "Are you going to be a lady and turn your back when I get out?" he asked with amusement, beginning to emerge from the water so that first his broad chest and then his hard, tapered waist became visible.

Sarah regarded his water-slick body. "And what if I don't?" she challenged, her hazel eyes beginning to spark mischievously.

"Then it won't be me who's embarrassed," he declared, taking another step forward so that his flat stomach was now exposed.

Hastily, Sarah turned around. "I'll meet you in the car," she threw over her shoulder.

An awkward silence hung in the air as they drove back. Sarah turned her head away from Matt to watch trees and catch brief glimpses of the coastline flashing past. But she wasn't really seeing any of the magnificent oceanside scenery. She was too preoccupied with what had just happened, or rather, not happened. She couldn't hide the truth from herself. Back there at the cove she had wanted Matt to pull her passionately into his arms. And because he hadn't, she was now aching with frustration. Yet, what could she say? She had told him she wasn't ready to continue the intimacy between them, and he had respected her wishes. He had been a gentleman, all right, too much of a gentleman. But she had set the rules, so how could she admit now that they were driving her crazy? He had said he wouldn't make love to her again until she was ready. Well, she now knew she was ready. Surely he must have sensed that back at the pool. Why hadn't he taken advantage of it? Was he going to make her tell him she wanted him? Sarah shot him a brief, resentful glance under her lashes. Telling him was something her pride simply wouldn't allow her to do.

As they pulled up in front of her house, she reached for the handle of the door. But before she could pull it open, Matt's hand shot out and covered hers.

"What's the trouble, Sarah?"

"Nothing," she mumbled.

But Matt wasn't fooled. "I know you too well for that. What are you angry about?"

"Nothing," she repeated stubbornly. What could she tell him, after all—that she was angry for having denied herself the satisfaction of his lovemaking? And even more absurd—that she was angry at Matt for abiding by her stated wishes?

Shaking herself loose from his grip, she scrambled out of the car and strode with quick steps up the path that led to her porch. Now she could feel Matt watching her. And so she deliberately did not turn and wave. It wasn't until she'd climbed the steps and opened the screen door that she heard his car pull away.

CHAPTER FIVE

So Matt was just going to drive off and leave her alone with the frustrated energy that was coursing directionlessly through her. Stepping into the house, she slammed the door with a force that rattled the windows. There was a certain satisfaction in the outburst, but it wasn't enough. Folding her arms tightly across her chest, she stood looking about the living room and tapping her foot.

What was she going to do with herself now? Running on the beach to work off some of this tension might be one solution. But Matt would surely see her and perhaps even guess the reason for it. If the house hadn't already been spotless, she might have grabbed a dust mop and released some of her frustration that way. But then Sarah slapped her forehead with an open palm in a gesture of self-reproach. What in the world was she thinking about? She had plenty of work to do. Her show in New York was only six weeks away now, and the major piece for it was still unfinished.

Racing up the stairs, she quickly stripped off the summery skirt and flowered blouse she'd worn for Matt and changed into the jeans and T-shirt that were her standard work uniform. Forcing her thoughts away from what had happened—or not happened—at the secluded cove, she began to concentrate her mental energy on *Dream Woman*.

Practically flying down the stairs, she strode purposefully through the kitchen and out into her studio where she shot a rueful glance at the driftwood dragon that had now become a friendly guardian over her creative efforts. It was almost like having a bit of Matt to watch over her. But right now it was hard to decide whether that was truly a benefit or not.

Thanks to her preoccupation with him, it had been almost a week since she'd looked at the half life-size sculpture, which was supposed to be the the centerpiece of her show. And when she unwrapped the protective plastic, she stood back to give it a critical inspection. Though she'd gotten more of what she wanted to convey in *Dream Woman*'s face, it still wasn't right. But all at once, as though the proverbial light bulb had gone off in her head, she knew precisely what the figure's expression should be.

Setting to work with deft fingers, she wet down the clay. And when the consistency was right, her hands began to mold the pliant material. Somewhere in her mind, she was astonished by the sureness of her touch. It was almost as though her hands were being guided. Afraid of losing the inspiration that was directing her, she forced the thought out of her mind. In the past she'd discovered that when she caught the wave of one of these creative urges, it was better to just ride it without self-conscious introspection. So totally absorbed was she in her task that the dinner hour slipped past and the natural light began to dim. It was only when the studio became a shadowy cavern that Sarah realized how late it was.

Flipping on the electric light, she blinked for a moment in the unaccustomed brightness and then stood back to look at what she had accomplished. Slowly her critical gaze traveled up the curving lines of the delicate female form before her. And then her eyes came to rest on the face. The slender neck was arched and the head was thrown back so that the luxuriant hair fell around the shoulders in abandoned disarray. But it was the face that

71

riveted Sarah's attention. Poignant longing and frustration were mirrored there for the world to see, and she knew that it had been her own tumultuous emotions that she had captured. For a moment Sarah was almost embarrassed by the self-revelation in the work. But then her pride in her art began to assert itself. It was good. She knew that beyond a doubt. It was probably the best thing she'd ever done. But an artist didn't necessarily create out of her own experience. Why should anyone assume that the yearning woman she'd brought forth from raw clay was really herself?

Suddenly Sarah felt completely drained. All the nervous energy that had spurred her to work without rest for the past few hours had now been dissipated, and she felt almost limp with exhaustion. Re-covering the figure, Sarah flipped off the light and walked with slow, dragging steps back into the kitchen. She needed to eat, and yet she didn't have the energy to fix herself a real meal.

Opening the refrigerator, she scanned the shelves for something appealing. Somehow nothing seemed right. And so, turning toward the pantry, she took out a jar of peanut butter, a crock of grape jelly, and a loaf of bread.

But when she brought her sandwich over to the table, the atmosphere in the kitchen seemed stale and oppressive. Reaching over, she unlocked the heavy, double-hung window in the breakfast area and pushed it open. The cool night air that streamed in was refreshing on her damp skin. And as she munched on the bread and peanut butter and jelly, she found her eyes turning toward the open, screened-in rectangle. She couldn't see Matt's house through the darkness. But she felt his presence. What was he doing? she wondered; certainly not having a thrown-together dinner like this, she guessed. There were a hundred things he might be doing. He might even be down on the beach now, stargazing.

All at once, shatteringly, the memory of what had happened between them there forced itself into her mind. Putting down the remains of her sandwich, she squeezed her eyes shut, as though that would protect her from the tide of longing that once again swept through her being. For a horrible moment she was tempted to leave the safety of her house and go to the beach to see if he really was there—to tell him she had changed her mind. But then reason reasserted itself. There was no way she was going to be so foolish as to seek him out and beg for his lovemaking. This afternoon she had wanted to blame him for his indifference. But the truth was that their present physical estrangement was really her choice, not his. And it had been a wise choice, too, she reassured herself. It was just that her body was refusing to be convinced.

With a weary sigh, she pushed her chair away from the table and stood up. All she wanted now was to go to bed and lose herself in the balm of sleep. But would she be able to do that? she wondered. Not on her own, she guessed.

Pausing once more at the refrigerator, she took out an open bottle of Chablis and poured herself a stemmed glassful. She often liked to relax with a glass of the pale vintage in the evening. And part of the small pleasure of the ceremony was to use one of the delicate crystal wine goblets that she'd inherited from her grandmother. Tonight the soothing liquid might help ease some of the tension that still lingered from the frustrations of the afternoon, she told herself as she slowly climbed the stairs to her bedroom.

After changing into her favorite long white cotton batiste gown, she brushed out her thick tresses until they hung in a luxuriant sweep around her bare shoulders. Turning off all the lights except the small, pink-shaded Tiffany lamp beside the bed, she settled herself comfortably in the cushioned rocker by the window. In the soft glow of the old lamp, she sat sipping the wine and rocking gently. And though she told herself she wouldn't think of Matt, her thoughts inevitably turned to him.

Out on the beach, a solitary figure paced back and forth. It might have given Sarah some small satisfaction to know that if she were feeling thwarted and alone, so was the man who walked with frustrated steps back and forth on the hard-packed sand. Like Sarah, his thoughts and emotions were in turmoil. There had been no question of turning away and breaking things off with Sarah. He couldn't do it. She had come to mean too much to him. So much, in fact, that he was even more terrified than ever of putting the relationship on the honest basis he should have established from the first. But like an avalanche set off by an innocent whisper, things had gotten out of hand before he could control them. For days now he'd been driven crazy by having her near and yet not feeling he could demand the intimacy he knew without doubt they both wanted.

Seeing her naked in that cove this afternoon like a shy water nymph had tested his self-control almost beyond endurance. Why had he ever suggested the crazy idea of swimming there? he asked himself. But he knew the answer. He had wanted to see her the way she was most beautiful. He had wanted to feast his starving eyes on the creamy perfection of her breasts, the seductive curve of her gently rounded hips, and the delicate white flesh of her thighs, which guarded the secret that had opened such loving pleasure to them both.

But, fool that he was, looking had not been enough. He had wanted to taste the pink buds of her breasts again, run his hands along the satin smoothness of her hip, and immerse himself in the beautiful secret of her femininity as he had that magic night on the beach. He had been aching with that want all afternoon and, as the hours passed, it had only gotten worse—not better.

Awhile ago he'd seen a dim light go on in the upstairs

window he knew was hers. He'd glimpsed her behind the shadowed glass once before, and now his heated imagination pictured her there waiting for him. Longingly, he lifted his eyes and stared at the lighted square reaching out to him like a beacon of hope to a drowning mariner. And then, as he watched, the light went off and the house was completely dark.

Sarah must be in bed now, he thought. And the image of her dear body lying soft and vulnerable in sleep was too much to bear. As though impelled by a will of their own, his feet began to take him across the moonlit stretch of sand and up the narrow cut from the beach that he'd come to know so well.

At the top, Sarah's house loomed like a dark castle. Indeed, he thought wryly, he had even provided the dragon that guarded the sanctity of its mistress. But tonight those high walls were a barrier to a need that was driving him beyond control. On stealthy feet, he approached the house, looking up at its windows and thinking only of the woman sleeping within.

He wanted her tonight, and the feelings driving him were so overwhelming that he could no longer fight them. He had been crazy to try to play this game. He knew that now. And yet, what could he do about it? In frustrated agitation, he prowled around the circumference of the house, staring with resentment at the heavy, locked doors and tightly shut windows. They might as well be the unbreachable defense system of a real castle, he told himself. For they were certainly keeping him away from the woman he wanted and needed tonight. In his desperate fantasy, he pictured himself breaking one of those barriers to get inside and it was only through heroic self-control that he didn't actually do it.

And then, abruptly his restless feet paused and his heart began to beat like a trapped eagle inside his chest. One of those windows was not closed after all. It was the one that

75

opened onto the kitchen, he surmised, picturing the interior of the room where he and Sarah had breakfasted only a few weeks before.

Unable to resist, he strode to the frame and tested the screen. It was old and almost fell out into his hands. What had Sarah been thinking, leaving it open like that? Anyone could get in. And it was lucky that he, and not someone dangerous, had discovered the breach.

Propping the screen against the side of the house, he placed his hands on the wide sill. With one easy motion, he hoisted his long, muscular body up. And then, pushing the sash open farther, he squeezed inside. It was not a maneuver that a man of his size could execute gracefully, especially since he landed in the middle of the claw-foot table. On the way down, he knocked over one of the Windsor chairs and held his breath after it hit the floor with a thud. But it was a big house, and the kitchen was at the opposite end from Sarah's bedroom. After a few moments he decided that she hadn't heard.

Without considering the irony of his gesture, Matt turned to lower the window and lock it for safety. Then he began to make his way through the lower part of the house toward the wide mahogany staircase in the front hall. Though he'd never climbed it before, he'd often dreamed of doing so. And now, in this strange fantasy mood that had overtaken him, he was going to make his fondest desires a reality.

The shadowy upstairs hall gave him no clues about which of the six closed doors branching off it led to Sarah's room. But the window he remembered was at the back left-hand corner of the house. And so he turned and headed for the end of the hall, his feet noiseless on the soft Oriental runner that padded the oak flooring.

But when he finally stood facing the door he surmised to be Sarah's, he paused. What in hell was he doing? he asked himself. He was already guilty of breaking and entering. And now he was going to invade Sarah's bedroom uninvited? Should he simply turn around, go back downstairs, and leave? But the longing that had driven him here and the way Sarah's passion-roused body had looked in the moonlight when they'd made love that night on the beach banished all doubts.

With a determined hand, he slowly turned the knob and pushed the door open. For a long moment he stood in the doorway, taking in the moonlight-silvered objects in the spacious, comfortably furnished room.

An old-fashioned four-poster bed dominated one wall. And as he tiptoed closer, he could see that it was occupied. In graceful disarray, Sarah lay on her back, her sleeping face turned up toward him. Her hair had been pulled back from her face this afternoon. But now it was spread in a dark curtain across the pillow, and one strap of her delicate white gown had slipped off her shoulder so that the soft curve of her breast was tantalizingly visible. The light sheet she'd thrown over herself was tangled around her legs. And he could see a provocative expanse of thigh peeking out where her gown had ridden up.

The vision of her vulnerable loveliness was too much for him to bear. Crossing the room in three strides, he gained the side of the bed and sat down gently. When the mattress gave with his weight, Sarah sighed and wriggled closer, as though sensing his presence.

The motion sent a lock of dark hair tumbling across her forehead. With gentle fingers he reached out to brush it back. And then, stroking the smooth skin, he bent down and brushed his lips lightly against her brow. Unable to restrain himself now, his hand moved from her hair, down the length of her throat to the delicate curve of her shoulder.

Sarah's lids fluttered open. And she stared up at him with eyes that were fathomless pools in the moonlight.

77

"God, Sarah, I couldn't stay away from you," he whispered huskily as his lips sought hers.

In answer she reached up, her fingers curling around the back of his neck to draw him down beside her on the bed.

Sarah was dreaming. For a long time before she'd finally tried to go to sleep, she'd sat in her bedroom, taking small sips of wine. But though the cool liquid had slipped down her throat like a balm, it hadn't turned her thoughts from Matt or eased the yearning that seemed to possess her body like an unquenchable thirst. There were so few unmixed pleasures in life. Almost everything required some sacrifice of freedom, integrity, or future pain. But while some things were not worth their price, others were. Sarah was beginning to think that the joy Matt's lovemaking might bring her now was worth any sacrifice she might later have to make in regret or heartbreak. And who was to say what lay in the future? Just because her marriage had been unsuccessful, that didn't necessarily doom her relationship with Matt. Oh, why had she sent him away this afternoon? Why hadn't she buried her damnable pride and neurotic doubts in order to tell him how she really felt and what she really wanted?

But it was too late now, she thought wearily as she switched off the light and lay down on the wide, empty bed. Though the sheets were cool, and the wind from the ocean coming in through the open window fanned her cheek, her flesh was heated with frustrated wants and needs—needs that only Matt could satisfy. But that was impossible now, she told herself. Would she ever be able to sleep tonight? she wondered.

Sarah had exhausted herself that afternoon, and the ceaseless ferment of her mind and body had compounded that weariness. Despite her agitation, the wine and the fresh sea air did its work. Sarah closed her eyes and drifted into a dream-filled sleep. But just as earlier her thoughts had been of Matt, so now were her dreams. Through the shadowy mists of her unconscious, he came toward her like a tall prince. The moonlight silvered his hair and the noble features of his face the way it had during their lovemaking on the beach. But though his gaze, fixed on her sleeping body, was dark and mysterious, she could feel the desire that burned in his eyes. It was a desire that matched her own.

In her dream vision, it was as though she lay on her bed, imprisoned in a spell. She could not move or speak but could only wait helplessly, aching for her lover to approach, but unable to urge him forward. What if he should turn away and leave her alone? The thought was torment. But mercifully, he did not retreat. Steadily, he came on. And then he was beside her, his hands touching her flesh, his lips grazing her fevered skin. The contact broke through the gossamer restraints of her dream vision. Finally, she was able to move.

"Matt, oh, Matt," she whispered on a sigh. And her hands went up to clasp themselves behind his neck and draw him closer. It was then that Sarah realized she was no longer asleep. This was not a beautiful dream, but an even more beautiful reality. "How . . ." she began to whisper tremulously.

But Matt's warm fingers on her lips silenced her. "I couldn't stay away." He gave a low, rueful laugh. "I climbed in your kitchen window because I was going crazy wanting you."

Her hands twined themselves in his thick hair, feeling the silvered strands curl themselves like an embrace around her eager fingers. "Oh, Matt, that's all I've been thinking about for hours—days, if I'm honest about it," she murmured. And it was so true. Every nerve ending in her body was alive with that unsatisfied craving.

With a groan Matt's face came down, his lips fusing

themselves to hers in a kiss that sealed their mutual longing.

"This afternoon at the cove," he finally whispered huskily, his warm breath a caress against her cheek, "I could hardly keep my eyes off you. You were so lovely, Sarah, so beautiful—like a naked goddess from the sea. I wanted to touch you, to feel the weight of your perfect breasts in my hands, to run my fingers along the outlines of your body. It nearly killed me to keep my hands off you."

"Touch me now," Sarah urged. She had wanted the same thing. Now she felt as though her body were on fire for him.

But instead of doing as she asked Matt drew back slightly, and she could see a small smile lifting the corners of his mouth. "I want to look at you," he told her quietly. "Let me see you the way you were this afternoon."

Though Sarah stared up at him wordlessly, he could read the consent in her face. Gently, he slipped the narrow straps of her gown down off her shoulders. And then he pushed away the soft material of her nightdress so that her breasts were free. For what seemed to Sarah like a long time, he merely gazed down at their white roundness, watching them tauten and swell as though his look were a caress. Then, slowly, his head lowered, and while his hands cupped their fullness, he reverently kissed both rosy, straining peaks.

Though they were already hard with yearning, when Matt began to suck gently on their tips and then trace a moist path along their perimeters with his tongue, pulsing currents of excitement sang inside Sarah's body. They coursed a tingling path to her abdomen, and then lower, where they seemed to gather in a frenzied knot.

Convulsively, Sarah's hands clutched at Matt's shoulders and then fluttered down the sides of his back to tug the shirt he wore out of the waistband of his slacks. She wanted to feel his bare skin beneath her fingers. And soon she had realized that goal. Slipping underneath the loosened barrier of his shirt, her hands moved up the powerful length of his back. Her fingertips reveled in the feel of his smooth skin and the bone and sinew that rippled beneath it.

But that was not enough. In a moment her fingers had traveled around to the front of his shirt where she began to slip the buttons out of their confinement. Understanding her purpose, he pulled away slightly and watched with glowing eyes as she slowly undid his shirt and pushed it back from his smooth, heavily muscled shoulders. When the upper part of his body was finally bare, she reached up and kissed the hard pebble of each flat male nipple, bestowing the same loving attention he'd given her.

When he felt her mouth on his flesh, Matt shuddered and then wrapped his hands around her back, pressing her close to him. For a moment he buried his face in the dusky curtain of her flowing hair. And then he whispered, "More, Sarah, I want more. Undo my jeans for me."

Her mouth dry with excitement, Sarah's trembling fingers moved down the length of his back again and then around to the front of his body where she could feel the firm skin of his chest and hard belly. Slowly, tantalizingly, her hands slid down that solid, flat surface until she came in contact once again with the waistband of his pants. But instead of unsnapping them immediately, her fingers slipped underneath the tight cloth, exploring with short, delicate strokes the hard flesh that strained beneath.

Matt gasped at her teasing invasions. "You're driving me crazy," he rumbled in her ear. "Help me take them off, for God's sake!"

Suddenly, Sarah was all compliance. Tugging the snap free, she began to push at the tight denim, but the stiff material was hard to maneuver. It was Matt who had to strip the covering from the lower part of his body. With one swift, impatient movement, he was suddenly naked before her in all his perfect masculine beauty. Sarah gazed at him hungrily. And then her eyes widened as she realized just how aroused he was.

"Yes," Matt growled tenderly. "I need you very badly tonight, Sarah. But not before you need me just as much." He knelt on the floor next to the bed and dropped soft kisses on her exposed breasts. "Oh, my beautiful one, let me make love to you now. I've been dreaming about doing this for days. Let me have my way."

Gently he pushed her back down on the bed. And then he drew her gown down until she was as naked as he. "I want to kiss you all over, every beautiful inch of you," he murmured as his lips once more sought her breasts.

Shivers of delight rippled through Sarah's body as his tongue paid homage once more to her already straining nipples and then began to move lower. Delicately, he caressed her rib cage and then her small, flat stomach. Like a hummingbird seeking nectar, his tongue dipped into the shallow well of her navel, making her shiver again and arch her pelvis in an inborn response of age-old feminine invitation.

Matt's large hands came down to grasp her hips and hold them still while his head moved down farther yet. Her response was even greater when his lips found the soft inner flesh of her thighs, nibbling a tantalizing path to the core of her femininity.

Seeking to make him understand her need, her own hands went down to his head, twining themselves amid the thick, fair strands and tugging gently. "Please, Matt," she moaned. "I want you so much I feel I'm going to burst!"

He chuckled low in his throat and slid his body up over hers. Once more she could look into his eyes to find her own overwhelming feeling of longing mirrored there. Sarah felt herself drowning with love and need for this man. Everything about him was dear to her: the strong, regular features of his intelligent face; his sun-bright hair;

his eyes, so green and promising now; and his long hard masculine body that was mastering hers so utterly.

"You can't need me more than I need you," he assured her, his voice thick with passion. Quickly he levered his length up and spread her legs so they could cradle his hips. His hand went down, stroking and fondling, feeling how ready Sarah was to receive his lovemaking.

She was trembling with anticipation, her hands clutching at the powerful muscles of his back.

And then, with an incredibly satisfying thrust, he was inside her, filling her completely, making her ache with the sensation of his total possession. Though it was hardly possible, Sarah's pelvis arched even farther as she tried to receive all of him.

But his hands on her soft buttocks stilled her. "I want to make love to you slowly," he whispered in her ear. "I want it to be perfect for you this time, Sarah."

As far as she was concerned, it was already perfect. But the care and concern Matt was showing her made tears come to her eyes. Oh, how she wanted this lover, wanted to hold him close forever!

Just as he had promised, Matt began to move within her slowly, delicately, building up a mounting pressure of desire that made her wriggle beneath him despite his insistence that she accept the leisurely pace he was setting. It was as though a heated coil were being gradually wound up to an unbearable tightness within her. The pressure had to be released. Her hands went to his thrusting buttocks, unconsciously clenching into their firm, tight contours to urge him on. But though Sarah's legs twisted beneath his with unsatisfied yearning and her mouth sought his throat where she kissed him fervently, Matt was determined to make her wait for the ultimate satisfaction. It was not until she was so ready that she thought she might detonate with the tension he had built, that he finally began to thrust with a power and speed that brought her over the edge of desire into dazzlingly complete fulfillment.

The tightly coiled spring suddenly unfurled like a whirling wheel in a fireworks display. Explosions of searing pleasure flashed hotly through her body, radiating from the feminine core so perfectly joined with Matt, to every part of her. Even her toes curled and then relaxed as the fantastic sensations streamed through her system.

When it was finally over, Sarah lay limp and relaxed under Matt's warm body, listening to the strong thrum of his heart and waiting while his rapid breathing gradually stilled. "Oh, God, Sarah, that was fantastic," he finally whispered in her ear.

Sarah's hands were resting loosely on his back. She joined them now, twining her fingers together so she could press him even more tightly to her body. "Matt, I've never been made love to so beautifully. It was wonderful!"

He lifted his head and smiled down tenderly at her. Sarah's response was to reach up and gently kiss the corners of his mouth.

"Let me stay here with you tonight," he asked. "I want to wake up in the morning with you beside me."

She nodded. "I wouldn't let you go now if you wanted to."

After he had pulled the sheet up over them, he hauled her close. "You must never leave your kitchen window open," he murmured gruffly into her ear before nibbling at it gently. "Someone might climb in and come up here to take advantage of you while you're defenseless and half-asleep."

"You're right, that would be terrible," Sarah retorted, beginning to drop tiny kisses down the side of his neck. She was aware, as she felt his lower body pressed to hers, of his returning ardor, and smiled secretly as she pressed her body more intimately to his.

CHAPTER SIX

It had been close to dawn before they fell asleep, wrapped in each other's arms. And so it was not until bright sunbeams slanted through her window that Sarah finally awakened. For a moment she was disoriented. And then when she turned her head and saw Matt sleeping beside her, memories of the previous night's joy flooded through her mind and body.

A slow smile spread across her features as her eyes dwelled on the magnificent expanse of Matt's tanned chest and the tumbled blond curls that framed his relaxed features. Earlier she might have gone to bed frustrated, but she certainly wasn't feeling that way now. The night had been the most fulfilling of her life. And from the faint smile of male satisfaction lifting Matt's lips, she surmised it had been satisfying for him as well.

But it wasn't just that beatific smile, of course. The soft words he had whispered to her through the night had told her much more. Sitting up in bed, Sarah turned slightly so that she could look down tenderly on Matt's relaxed form.

Yesterday afternoon she had been afraid he didn't want her. Now she knew beyond a doubt that nothing could be further from the truth. Their week together had left Matt yearning for her as much as she was for him. But she no longer intended to hold herself back from him. In fact, that would be impossible, she knew, bending to graze his muscled shoulder with a light kiss.

Last night had brought her the kind of physical fulfillment that most women only fantasize about. Yet it had meant much more than just the sating of a physical need. It was time to be honest with herself for a change. She was falling in love with Matt Lyons.

And from his impassioned lovemaking, she dared to hope that he returned those feelings.

Just then Matt stirred beside her, and she turned to watch as he stretched out a long, muscular arm as though searching for her in his sleep.

For a moment she was tempted to snuggle down next to him once more. But she was fully awake now, and the bright sunlight told her the morning was far advanced. It would be fun to wake Matt up with a really elaborate breakfast, she thought. The last time she'd fixed him one, it had just been cold cereal and fruit. But now she wanted to make their first real morning together as memorable as the night before—though that was impossible, she thought, unable to suppress a grin. Did he like blueberry and lemon muffins? she wondered. They were one of her specialties. With homemade strawberry jam and omelets they should do quite nicely.

As Sarah swung her slim legs over the side of the bed and slipped her feet into her favorite wooden-heeled mules, she realized she was ravenous. She hadn't been this hungry in weeks, she thought, grinning again as she realized that last night's tumultuous lovemaking was probably the cause. And if she was hungry, Matt was sure to be starved when he woke up.

But he was sleeping so peacefully now that she didn't want to disturb him until it was necessary. And besides, she wanted the gourmet breakfast to be a surprise. Matt didn't even know she could cook, and what better way to enlighten him than to reappear in the bedroom bearing a tray loaded with a morning's feast for two.

Slipping into her white eyelet robe, she tiptoed quietly

down the wide stairs and into the kitchen. The sun was lighting all the surfaces of the high-ceilinged room, giving it a freshness and sparkle that she didn't remember from the day before. Or was it just her happy state of mind that made everything seem beautiful this morning? Smiling, Sarah glanced at the window Matt had climbed through last night. He was right, of course. Under ordinary circumstances, she should never have left it open. But she was very glad she had last night.

Humming to herself, she set a pot of coffee on the stove and then opened the refrigerator to take out milk and eggs. Next she turned to the pantry for flour. In a few minutes she had mixed up a golden batter, added blueberries and grated lemon rind, and started to fill muffin cups. She was just scraping the bowl in an attempt to eke out one more muffin when she heard the familiar clank of the mail slot in the front hall. It was a sound that never failed to catch her attention. When she was a child, collecting the letters and bringing them to the big, old-fashioned mahogany sideboard in the dining room had been her special job. And although she now received more junk mail than anything else, she still looked forward to what the day might turn up.

Opening the oven, she quickly popped the muffin pans inside and glanced at the clock so she'd know when to take them out. Then she went out into the hall to scoop up the envelopes that now lay in a heap on the floor under the mail slot. As she leafed through the small stack, she smiled when she recognized her sister Bev's distinctive scrawl and fanciful pink-and-white envelope. Bev was a junior at Berkeley, majoring in sociology. The difference in their ages had made it hard to be friends while the two of them were growing up. But now that her little sister was in college, they were developing a closer relationship. Bev wrote periodically to report on her academic progress and her fiancé, who was also a classmate. He was the reason

87

why she'd elected to spend the summer in school rather than on the Cape with Sarah.

As she walked back toward the kitchen, Sarah began opening Bev's envelope. But she was momentarily distracted by the enticing smell of fresh-brewed coffee from the pot on the stove.

After pouring herself a cup, she glanced at the time. The muffins wouldn't be done for several minutes, so she'd be able to start Bev's letter while she sipped her coffee and waited.

The first part was the usual cheerful nonsense her sister customarily sent—paeans of praise for her fiancé, Greg, the latest university gossip, and an account of a recent rock concert. But on the second page was an almost off-hand reference to a man named Matt Lyons. And as Sarah read it, her heart seemed to stop beating, and she went cold all over.

"He's a film producer who wants to do some kind of documentary on Daddy. The guy was a real sweet-talking hunk, and I might have succumbed to his charms, but I was deep into midterms when he showed up. And then there's Greg. You know how jealous he is. He came around one afternoon when Lyons was waiting to see me and almost blew his stack. Sorry I didn't warn you earlier. I know how hyper you are about discussing Dad with the media, although I'm not sure I go along with you all the way on that. But I had a research project and couldn't get to anything else for weeks.

"Lyons was pretty persistent, and he may just show up on the Cape. But I'm not worried about your ability to handle him; I know his type leaves you cold."

The letter went on to other topics. But Sarah was not

capable of taking it in. All she could do was read those horrifying two paragraphs over and over while her numbed brain tried to assimilate their meaning.

The hand that held the pink-and-white, butterfly-etched stationery began to tremble.

What a colossal joke Matt had played on her, Sarah thought as she read that last ironic sentence once again. He had used his looks and charm like an angler dangling a brightly feathered lure in front of a hungry fish. And she had certainly swallowed the bait.

The thought brought a fiery flush to her cheeks. Last night she had opened up to him in a way she never had with any man before. She had given him not only her body but her mind and heart as well. And all the time when she'd been imagining that he felt as she did, he'd only been playing her for a fool.

She was so wrapped up in her thoughts that it took several minutes for the smell of burning muffins to penetrate to her consciousness. By the time it did, the smoke was beginning to wisp from the oven. A half hour ago she had invested a lot of love and effort in those muffins. But now she was glad they were ruined. Switching off the heat, she opened the door and peered inside at the charring lumps that would have been the centerpiece of Matt's surprise breakfast. With a pot holder she fished out the pan and dumped it into the sink before turning on the cold water.

The ruined muffins were a perfect metaphor for her own feelings. All the tender illusions about Matt she'd cherished this morning had been completely destroyed, leaving a charred residue of anger. Their lovemaking of the night before seemed like nothing but a mockery, and she was the object of that cruel laughter.

Picking up the letter, Sarah turned on her heels and marched out of the kitchen. With her lips set in a grim line, she climbed the stairs toward her bedroom. All she

89

could think of was getting that lying bastard, Matt Lyons, out of her bed and out of her life.

When she reached the room's threshold, however, the sight of him stopped her cold. He was still asleep, his golden hair tangled from her fingers and his handsome mouth still curved in a boyishly contented smile. He looked exactly the same as when she'd slipped out of bed to make him breakfast. But now the sight of his golden good looks only made Sarah want to wipe that satisfied expression off his face. Striding forward, she curled her fingers in the sheet and yanked it off the bed. Suddenly Matt's naked body was completely exposed. His eyes snapped open, and he stared up groggily into her face.

"What . . ." he began. And then he caught the murderous expression in Sarah's eyes, and his forehead began to wrinkle. "What is it, baby?" he asked.

If that were possible, the term of endearment magnified her rage. "Don't baby me, you bastard!" she spat out, hands on her hips and hazel eyes flashing fire. "Get the hell out of my bed and out of my house. I never want to see you again!"

Matt stared at her in openmouthed astonishment. "What is it?" he finally managed again.

In answer, Sarah threw Bev's letter at him. "That ought to explain what the 'matter' is," she ground out. "It's from my sister—the one you tried to get around at Berkeley a few weeks ago."

Matt went white under his tan as comprehension dawned. "Sarah, you've got to believe . . ." he began.

But she didn't want to hear any of his lying explanations. Picking up his jeans where he'd dropped them on the floor the night before, she hurled them in the general direction of his chest. "Get yourself decent and get out of here," she hissed.

"Sarah," he appealed again.

But she wanted to hear no more from him. Casting one

last, scathing glance in his direction, she stalked from the room. She was pacing up and down the kitchen when he joined her. He hadn't bothered to put his shirt or his shoes on and was dressed only in the pants she'd thrown at him. In his hand, Bev's letter was held in a white-knuckled grip.

"Sarah, I've read this," he began, dropping the letter on the kitchen table as though it were a viper. "I know it sounds bad."

Sarah paused by the sink and stared at him with narrowed eyes. She had no intention of holding a discussion with him. He had tricked her, and she wasn't going to let him do it again. "Isn't it true that you arranged to bump into me on the beach because you wanted to wheedle information about my father out of me?"

Matt's face began to turn a dull red. "All right. I wouldn't put it exactly that way. But it was more or less true in the beginning," he admitted. "But—"

Sarah had heard more than enough. She didn't let him finish. "I told you to get out of here, and I meant it. You've done nothing but lie to me from the first, and I never want to see you again."

"Sarah, after last night you can't really mean that," Matt pleaded, starting forward. His arms were outstretched, and she knew that he intended to get around her the way he always had in the past, with his body. But he had taken the wrong tack. Bringing up last night was like rubbing salt in an open wound. The thought of his laying a hand on her now was more than she could bear, and she was suddenly desperate to stop him. Swiveling in a defensive reaction, she grabbed the first thing that came to her hand. It happened to be the pan full of soggy, charred muffins.

Without thinking, she hurled the pan and its contents at the advancing man. The edge of the tin caught him painfully in the chest before clattering to the floor. And its payload of soggy, blackened missiles scattered like buckshot before falling to the floor around his feet in charred little heaps.

For a moment, both of them stood frozen in disbelief. Sarah stared in horror at what her out-of-control emotions had caused her to do. The line where the narrow edge of the pan had hit him was already beginning to turn an angry red. He would have a painful welt there, she realized, but he didn't even seem aware of it now.

It was Matt who moved first. Looking down at his body, be began to brush the remains of the fusillade from his skin. "Whatever you think I've done to you, I don't believe I deserved that, Sarah," he began. "In fact, I don't think I deserve a lot of the treatment I've been getting from you. Ever since we met, I've been tiptoeing around your unpredictable emotions. One minute you blow hot and the next minute you blow cold. Well, I've had about all I can take."

"Good," Sarah whispered hoarsely, "because all I want is for you to get out of here and out of my life." As she spoke, her hand was fumbling on the counter for something else to use as a defensive weapon.

Seeing what she was about, Matt crossed the room quickly and seized her arms. Pulling them behind her back, he held her tightly against his body so that she couldn't move.

"I think you're too confused to know what you want," Matt grated. "But I'm not about to let you use me for target practice again." Although his words were spoken with a deadly calm, it was obvious that his own anger was beginning to rise to the surface.

But the way he was restraining her, while speaking as though she were some sort of obstreperous child, only added fuel to her own indignation. "Get your hands off me, you, you mealymouthed hypocrite! I'll bet you make a habit of exploiting women this way. You've certainly got it down to a science."

92

Matt's expression darkened. "Stop behaving like a bratty child throwing a fit. Are you trying to bring our relationship down to the level of a Punch and Judy show?"

"If that's what it takes to get you out of here—" she began, but his thunderous look stopped her.

"Sarah, let's keep on the subject. You just accused me of being an expert at exploiting women. That's ridiculous. The reason I didn't tell you about my film project was that I was afraid it might jeopardize what we had together . . ."

She didn't want to listen to any more of his lies. The iron bands of his arms held her upper body immobile. But she could still move her legs. Glaring up at him with fierce defiance, she brought her heel down squarely on one of his bare feet.

Though Matt yelped in pain, the effect of her attack was not what she expected. Instead of releasing her, his steely grip tightened menacingly on her arms. And then he shifted his hold so that he could raise her up off the floor. In the next minute she was head to head with him, her feet dangling helplessly. Matt stared directly into her eyes, his nose only inches from hers.

"Don't you ever do anything like that to me again," he warned.

Sarah couldn't help being frightened at the results of her own reckless behavior. Though it had all been a masquerade, she'd never seen him as anything except a gentle and persuasive lover. But now, as his green eyes glared into hers like a furious jungle cat's, she wondered somewhere in the back of her mind if she'd made a serious error.

But before her rage could turn to fear, Matt had set her back down on the floor as though she were a sack of potatoes. "I can see it would be pointless to try to hold a rational discussion with you now," he bit out. Turning, he started toward the screen door. Sarah noticed with some small satisfaction that he was limping.

As soon as he'd gained the porch, she slammed the door behind him and locked it.

Leaning back against it, she took a deep breath. But it was going to take more than a few deep-breathing exercises to bring back her equilibrium. Her heart was racing like a greyhound. She gazed around the empty kitchen, seeing nothing except the scene that had just rocked it. It was several minutes before her gaze finally focused on the gooey mess that had once been her love offering to Matt.

Not only had he made a mess of her life, but also of her kitchen, she fumed irrationally. And he wasn't going to have to clean up either one. That was going to have to be her job—just as it had been her job to get her life back in order after the disaster of a marriage with Brad was finally over. She had sworn that would never happen to her again. She had promised herself that she would never let a man use her for his own purposes. But Matt had made her forget all her good sense. Like a fool, she'd been taken in again. And now she was going to have to pay the price.

Although the muffins had made a disaster of her clean floor and walls, they were going to be a much easier mess to deal with, she thought bitterly, kneeling down and beginning to scrape charred crumbs from the tile.

Thirty minutes later she had wiped the last traces of Matt Lyons's aborted breakfast off her kitchen floor and walls. But she felt little satisfaction. Restless energy still coursed through her body. Jumping from the floor, she crossed to the trash can and disposed of the dirty cloth she'd been using. If only she could as easily dispose of every trace of the man himself. And then her mind suddenly pictured him as he'd appeared in the kitchen. He'd been wearing only his jeans. That meant his shirt, shoes, and socks were still up in her bedroom. Sarah's jaw hardened and she turned toward the stairs. Maybe she couldn't get him out of her mind, but she could certainly get any reminders of him that were left out of her house. And that included that damned piece of driftwood that had started all this, she told herself ten minutes later as, dressed now in shorts and a T-shirt, she unceremoniously stuffed his clothing into the garbage and emptied the kitchen trash on top of it for good measure.

Following the path around the side of the house, she stopped when she reached the window of her studio. There, gazing serenely at her with the gnarled wood indentations that looked so much like eyes, was Eustace. Up until today, when she'd passed this way, he'd seemed like a friend guarding her domain and welcoming her, too. But now she felt as though he were mocking her.

Flinging open the screen door, she marched inside and grabbed the twisted piece of driftwood. Matt, of course, had been the one to carry it in. At the time she'd assumed that his protestations about its weight had simply been a ploy to get inside the house. But in that, at least, he hadn't been lying. The natural sculpture was surprisingly heavy and unwieldy. And it took her quite a bit of effort to wrest it from its perch.

Staggering under its ungainly burden, she pushed through the door and down toward the beach, stopping several times to set it down so she could massage the ache in her arms. There would have been no way she could carry it to the distant spot where she'd first seen it. But she was able to drag it down through the cut and to the water's edge. Fortunately the tide was high and the water would be going out soon. Kicking off her sandals, Sarah waded out into the water, cradling the dragon in her arms. When she judged she'd carried it out deep enough, she dumped it in the water and then turned and started back to shore. But when she glanced over her shoulder, she was startled to see that, instead of drifting out to sea, it seemed to be following her back to shore. Apparently she'd made a

95

miscalculation about the tide. With every swell, the maddening beast moved closer to the spot where she'd entered the water. And what's more, his gnarled wood eyes seemed to be staring at her accusingly.

Sarah stood for a moment with her hands on her hips, regarding the beast in exasperation. As she watched, it drifted closer until finally its head butted gently against her stomach. Sarah struggled with a whole raft of mixed emotions. Part of her was irritated and half-inclined to drag the creature out into the water again. But another part of her was glad the little beast had refused to be cast away so easily. She had grown fond of Eustace, and she knew that she would find the window of her studio empty without him. Anyway, throwing him away was really silly. Why should she take out her anger at Matt's perfidy on an innocent inanimate object?

Sighing, she put her hand on its head and began to guide it back to shore. And a few minutes later she was clasping its damp body to her chest and trudging back up the cut. Strangely, even though it was wet now, it seemed less of a burden than it had on the way down.

CHAPTER SEVEN

Over the next few days, Sarah found that getting the rest of her life in order again was much more difficult than deciding what to do about Eustace. She had to get back on course but didn't know quite how. Despite herself, half her waking hours seemed to be spent thinking of Matt.

A visit to the village nearby didn't help either. When she went into the post office for a roll of stamps, Mr. Robinson, who had known her since she was a child, commented on the "nice young feller who's been asking questions about your father."

"What kind of questions?" Sarah wanted to know, her eyes narrowing.

Mr. Robinson stamped a package first class and dumped it in the canvas bin at his elbow. "Oh, not the usual stuff. He seems to know all about your parents and the accident. But he was interested in anything I might remember about your dad when he was growing up here."

"Was he blond and good-looking?" Sarah bit out, feeling her heart begin to pound in her chest.

When the postmaster recognized the brief description, she felt her jaw tighten. So, Matt Lyons knew all about the accident, did he? She might have guessed. At the time, the questions he'd asked *her* had seemed innocent enough. But now she knew better. That had all been part of his act.

As she spent the morning doing all the errands she'd put off in the last week so she could spend more time with

97

Matt, several other villagers echoed what Mr. Robinson had told her. Matt was obviously not sitting at home pining because he'd lost her. No, indeed, he was putting his time to good use—prying into all the details of her family life that he hadn't managed to wheedle out of her. And the damnable part was that no one else knew what a self-serving hypocrite he really was. He'd charmed the townspeople just as effortlessly as he'd charmed her. And what could she do about it? She couldn't tell them her side. It would only make her look like a gullible fool.

All this was confirmed by her visit to Mrs. Crumly's grocery store. The kindly old lady, who had been supplying the village with staples for the past half century, approached Sarah just as she had finished filling her cart. "Oh, there you are," she crowed. "I was just talking about you to that nice boy renting the Bowers's cottage. My, what a good-looking young man, and so well mannered!" she added, beaming broadly.

"Oh, yes, indeed," Sarah agreed, not letting her expression change by a flicker. Matt was nothing if not well mannered. And charming. He could coax honey from a bear if he wanted to.

"That boy spent the whole morning with me yesterday," the little white-haired proprietress went on. And then she chuckled. "It was a real treat. You know, I haven't had a handsome young man pay so much attention to me since I ran a canteen in World War I."

It was really hard for Sarah to keep from grinding her teeth. She knew exactly how attentive Matt Lyons could be when he was after something. "Well, what did the two of you find to talk about?" she forced herself to ask sweetly.

Mrs. Crumly was nothing if not forthright. "Why, we talked about you and your father, dear," she volunteered as she began to load Sarah's groceries into a paper sack.

"Well, that sounds pretty dull," Sarah fished.

"Not to me, dear," Mrs. Crumly assured. "Your family has always been a colorful part of this town's history. That young man was fascinated with all my stories about old times like when you and your father used stop by and get supplies for a surprise picnic. Or when the two of you came in third in the yacht club race. And we had a good laugh over that time when you were learning to roller-skate and didn't know how to stop. Do you remember you plowed right into Mr. Sturgess and bounced off his spare tire?"

Sarah grimaced. She remembered all right. And the idea of Matt having access to such personal moments rankled. Just what was he going to do with the information? Was the whole world going to be seeing it on television in a few months?

"You and your dad were always so close. I know it must have been hard for you after that boating accident," Mrs. Crumley was saying.

Sarah nodded numbly. It had been hard. But the worst thing was finding out her father's life had been a lie, and that the family relationship she had treasured had been a sham. For most of his married life he'd been carrying on a torrid love affair with another woman. As a child she'd assumed his work was responsible for his frequent absences. But the letters from Marjorie Winter that she'd found in his Hollywood condominium after her parents' death had shown her otherwise.

Suddenly, all Sarah wanted was to get away from Mrs. Crumly's curious inspection and back to the safety of her house. Quickly, she fumbled in her purse for some bills. But before she could lay them on the counter, the old woman placed a gnarled hand over hers.

"I'm sorry if I brought up a subject that's painful to you, dear. But you can't spend all your life mourning the past. It's the present that counts. Take that young Matt Lyons, for example. When he spoke about you his voice

was so warm. Count your blessings that you've met someone like that."

Sarah stared speechlessly at the old woman. And then,
mumbling the first noncommittal reply that came to mind,
she snatched up her two grocery bags and fled. But, outside in the car, she couldn't flee from her thoughts.

Knowing that Matt was sleuthing around town, prying
into her family's private affairs was bad enough. But if he
found out about the business with Marjorie Winter it
would be a hundred times worse. She knew now that Matt
was unscrupulous. He wouldn't hesitate to use that kind
of unsavory material in his documentary, making her father's private indiscretions a hot topic. Since reading her
father's letters, Sarah had been living with memories that
now mocked her. Those letters had seen to that. Sarah set
her jaw. She hadn't even shared those letters with her
sister. They were her secret, she told herself defiantly. No
one, least of all Matt Lyons, was going to find out what
was in them.

Unwittingly, Mrs. Crumly had stirred up all the troubled feelings that Sarah had been trying to suppress. When
she got back home, her insides were still churning. But
with a discipline she'd learned from years of effort, she
forced herself to get some work done in the studio. It was
a blessing that *Dream Woman* was finally finished to her
satisfaction. Now she could begin the less demanding
work of readying it for casting in bronze.

Sarah worked herself mercilessly through the rest of the
day. And that night she fell exhausted into bed. Despite
her fatigue of the night before, she awoke just before dawn.
Since her parting with Matt, she'd given up her morning
run. And that was probably part of the problem, she told
herself. She needed the workout to keep up her energy.
This morning, since she was already awake, she might as
well take advantage of the situation.

Pulling on her jogging outfit, she headed quickly down

100

to the beach. But as she reached the base of the cut, she stopped short. Spread out before her on the dry sand was an amazing collection of pebbles, seaweed, driftwood, and seashells. For a moment she stared at the strange arrangement in openmouthed disbelief. The small natural objects had been painstakingly and artfully formed into a message which read, "Give me another chance."

Even without a signature, she knew very well who had assembled this strange collage. It was Matt, of course. It must have taken him hours to collect all these little bits and pieces from the beach. And the message itself must have taken more hours of painstaking work in the dark the night before. Had he used a flashlight? she wondered. Stepping closer, she gazed down at the swirling, graceful letters, so cunningly formed out of such unlikely material. He had never talked to her about his profession, of course. But his artistic talent was obvious from the work at hand. There was no doubt that he was a man of many abilities, she thought. But one of them was his gift for persuasion. And that one wasn't going to work on her again.

With her jaw set, she gave the words several good kicks that sent the bits of driftwood and shells flying in all directions. She was about to continue on to the beach when she stopped short again.

My God, Matt was probably out there waiting to see what her reaction to his peace offering would be. Well, he'd find that out soon enough, she thought, turning around and stamping back up the cut to her house.

Grimly she switched on the radio to a rock and roll station and began doing sit-ups on the living room floor. She might not be able to run. But she had to work off her agitation somehow.

When she finished, there was a fine sheen of sweat all over her body. But the exercise session wasn't enough to banish the specter of Matt Lyons from her mind. Today, it wasn't quite so easy to work. And in fact, she found herself ruining an experimental casting of a small sculpture.

By midmorning, she was about ready to quit when the phone rang. Sarah hesitated. Could it be Matt? And then she strode toward the phone, disgusted with herself. He had already made her wary of going down to the beach. She wasn't going to let him keep her from answering her own phone. If he were calling, she could simply slam the receiver down in his ear.

As it turned out, it wasn't Matt. It was her agent, Gordon Wentworth.

"I haven't heard from you in ages, darling," he began in a slightly accusing tone of voice.

"I, uh, I've been busy," Sarah hedged.

"Well, I guess I'm glad to hear that, since your show is so close. How's it been going?"

Sarah made a face at the phone. In the past she'd rather enjoyed having Gordon call to check up on her. It meant somebody cared. But now she couldn't help being slightly irritated by his possessive attitude. Besides, she was behind schedule. And she didn't care to listen to his scolding. "Things are going as well as can be expected," she hedged carefully.

"Does that mean you've finished that big important piece we discussed?"

"I'm in the middle of casting it now," Sarah assured him. "And I think you'll be pleased when you see it." That, at least, she felt confident of. So far *Dream Woman* was her one solid achievement in this mess of a summer.

"Can't wait to see it. Frankly, I can't wait to see its creator more. I've missed you, Sarah."

When she didn't answer immediately, he added, "Have you missed me?"

Sarah drew a blank. The truth was she hadn't even thought of Gordon since Matt Lyons had appeared on the

102

beach. But she knew enough about the male ego to realize she couldn't admit to that.

"Um . . ." she answered, hoping the noncommittal syllable could be interpreted for "yes."

Apparently he was willing to settle for that. "I'm counting the days until you get to New York," he told her before finally hanging up.

After carefully replacing the receiver in its cradle, Sarah snatched up a pillow from the sofa and hurled it across the room.

"Damn Matt Lyons," she grated. Before he'd forced his way into her life, she'd thought that maybe it was possible that she and Gordon might eventually get together. And, in fact, if she'd let him persuade her, it would have happened long ago. But now she knew that was impossible. She felt affection toward Gordon. But that was all. It was nothing like the explosive passion she'd known with Matt. And now she could never settle for the lukewarm feelings that Gordon Wentworth generated. That would be like going from vintage champagne to a flat beer. For a moment, amused at the fanciful comparison, her mouth curled. But her expression sobered quickly. It was no joke. Matt had opened up a door to a realm of intense sensuality and deep emotion that she'd never before even known existed. And that made it all the more cruel that he'd slammed it shut again. For now she felt like a child shivering outside in the cold.

The image stuck with her throughout the rest of the day and even into the sleepless night. By the next morning she told herself that she couldn't allow this situation with Matt to make a shambles out of her life. The meaningful relationship she'd thought she could build with the man might be impossible now, but she wasn't going to let him keep her from running on the beach, and she wasn't going to let him keep her from working. Today was going to be different from yesterday.

103

Defiantly, she pulled on her jogging shorts and then headed down to the beach. To her relief, the debris from Matt's elaborate collage had been cleared away. Maybe from now on he was going to leave her alone. But why did that thought leave her more depressed than ever? she asked herself as she started to trot along the sandy surface.

She had only gone fifty yards when she stopped short. On the hard-packed sand directly in her path was another collage. This one was more a picture than a message. Small natural objects were arranged to form a heart broken in two. And between the two jagged images was the word "Please."

It was hard not to be affected. And what was she to make of the message? Was Matt trying to tell her that his heart was broken? That hardly seemed possible.

Taking a more careful look at the picture, Sarah couldn't help but note how close it was to the lapping waves. Soon the tide would be coming in to sweep it away. Matt must have placed it in such a vulnerable position to save her the trouble of destroying it herself. Somehow, that knowledge was the hardest to deal with, and Sarah felt a lump form in her throat. Despite herself, she couldn't bear the idea of the whole thing being washed out to sea. Stooping quickly, she picked up one of the shells and stuffed it in her pocket. And then, before the tears that stung the back of her eyes blinded her completely, she turned and started to jog again, but in the other direction so that she would not encounter Matt's message on her way back.

So much for not letting Matt interfere with her day, she told herself, when she finally walked into her studio later that morning. Well, it wasn't going to happen again. She was going to start the initial firing on the last batch of pieces for the show. And she was going to give it her full attention. She didn't need a repeat performance of the blueberry muffin fiasco. Green ware was fragile and, if she let her mind wander, there was no telling what would happen.

Slowly, she loaded the kiln, making sure that none of the pieces touched each other or the walls. Then she closed the heavy, insulated lid and set the temperature. It took only a few minutes for the heat to begin building up. And with it came a feeling of satisfaction at seeing the last of her pieces on the way to completion. They represented weeks, in some cases, months, of work.

But as she stood looking musingly at the heating kiln, the feeling of being watched made her whirl around. Matt was standing at the door behind her, looking at her with a quizzical expression. Instantly, despite herself, she took in every detail of his appearance. His face was the same handsome collection of features, and yet he looked different. There were dark circles under his eyes and he seemed thinner.

"I saw you take Eustace down to the beach and out into the water last week," he said.

Sarah's gaze skidded away from his. "So?"

He sighed and shifted his weight. "So, you didn't throw him away after all. That gave me something to hope for."

Sarah's mouth set stubbornly. "How I treat an innocent piece of driftwood and my attitude toward a man who's made a fool of me have nothing to do with each other. Why are you here, Matt? I told you I didn't want to see you again."

"I'm here because I want to see you, and I think it's time you listened to my side of things. You owe me that much."

Sarah shook her head. "I don't owe you a thing."

Matt sighed again and brushed a weary forearm across his damp forehead. "It's hotter in here than the last time you had that thing on." He gestured toward the kiln. "And you don't even have the top propped open the way you did before."

Sarah gasped, and then her head swerved around sharply. He was right. She had forgotten to prop the lid. She looked at her watch; it had only been a few minutes and so there was a chance the green ware wasn't yet ruined. Where had her mind been when she'd made such a beginner's mistake? Grabbing a pair of heavily padded mitts, she quickly pulled the lid up and cringed back from the blast of superheated air that billowed out of the opening.

Matt seized her shoulders, but she only ducked her head out of the way and held stubbornly to the kiln.

"What are you trying to do?" he demanded.

"Quick, shove one of those firebricks underneath," she hissed, shaking her head at a stack of them on the floor.

Without further questions, he complied, swiftly inserting the brick under the heavy closure. The moment it was in place, he pulled Sarah away.

"What are you trying to do to yourself? Has that hot air burned your face?" Turning her around, he inspected her skin intently. "It doesn't look as if you've done any damage, but you'd better come out of this oven and let me put a cool cloth on it just to make sure."

"Really, I don't need . . ." Sarah began. But he was already guiding her firmly toward the sink. Finding a clean towel, he wet it and placed it gently over the feverish surface of Sarah's face.

He was right, she had to admit as she held the cloth to her cheeks. The cool wetness was soothing. But she felt like a fool. In her distracted state of mind, she'd almost ruined months of work. "Thank you," she finally said, taking the cloth away from her face. "If you hadn't mentioned the door, I would have lost a lot of really valuable pieces. I don't know how I could have done something so stupid."

Matt took her hand. "We all make stupid mistakes, Sarah, and I made one with you. Will you let me tell you about it now?"

106

Sarah stiffened at the reference to their relationship. She had told herself she didn't want to hear anything Matt Lyons had to say. But now, she was in his debt. She had told him to stay away. But if he hadn't come into her studio when he did, she would have had to throw away everything that was in the kiln this morning.

Denying him an opportunity to give his side of the story now would make her feel like an ingrate.

"All right," she finally conceded.

"Not here," he said, looking around at the studio. "Let's sit down in the living room."

Sarah looked at him suspiciously. Was he planning to try to sweet-talk her the way he had before? No matter how much she might want to pretend differently, she was still susceptible to him physically—and emotionally. Even as he stood before her, it was a struggle to keep from reaching out to touch the bronze skin of his arm. But he was already heading down the hall toward the front of the house. As she followed him along the passage, she watched him warily. But when they reached the living room, he sat down in an overstuffed chair and gestured for her to take the one opposite.

However, now that he had achieved part of his objective, he seemed reluctant to continue. Up until that morning when she'd gotten the fateful letter from her sister, he'd always seemed so much in control of the situation between them. Now he looked unsure of himself. And that was out of character.

Sarah told herself that he was simply deciding on the best strategy for getting something more out of her, after having won some small advantage in her studio. But when she took in the distress in his green eyes and the drawn look of his face, holding onto that cynical attitude was almost more than she could manage.

Yet, as the silence stretched painfully between them, Sarah stubbornly refused to break it. After all, Matt was the one who'd asked for this chance to explain himself. And she certainly wasn't going to play the gracious hostess and help him out.

Finally, looking at her with troubled eyes, he began to speak. "Sarah, I'd give anything if I could have told you myself that I was making a film about your father. I know how traumatic it was getting the information in a letter from your sister."

Sarah didn't bother to answer. Her reaction to the letter had been all too obvious.

"But try to understand it from my point of view. Yes, I came here to get information for my documentary. And I was on the beach because I wanted to meet you."

Sarah's lips pressed together as she listened. She'd known that, too. But that didn't make hearing it from Matt any less painful.

Sensing her feelings, he went on quickly. "But everything changed when I met you. You have to believe that. I suddenly wanted to get to know you because of yourself. That first day in your studio I realized there could be something very special between us. But I'd heard how protective you were of your privacy. And I was afraid that when you learned about my film, you'd misinterpret my motives—just as you've done."

"Misinterpret," Sarah echoed. "How could that be? You've just admitted that you wanted to find out about my father from me."

"I won't deny that. All I'm saying is that there was a lot more to it. I should have told you right away. But the longer I waited, the harder it was to do. You'd come to mean so much to me. But believe it or not, I intended to do it that morning after we'd spent the night together. It was the worst kind of bad luck that you found out before I had a chance to tell you myself."

"Just how did you intend to tell me, and what did you think my reaction would be?" Sarah whispered.

Matt stood up, jammed his hands in his pockets, and paced the length of the large Oriental rug. "I'd hoped that you cared enough for me to give me a decent hearing. I'd hoped that after we'd made love that way, you'd trust me enough to hear me out. I guess that's why I got so upset after you threw that pan at me. But I said some pretty rough things, as I recall. And I know I owe you an apology. If this meeting doesn't settle anything else, at least I've had the chance to say I'm sorry for that."

Sarah felt as though her throat had closed. It was hard enough to breathe, let alone say anything. So once again she remained silent.

"Is the apology accepted?" he finally asked.

Sarah nodded. They had both said some pretty hateful things that morning. But she knew that her harsh words and angry actions had provoked his strong response.

For a long moment, neither of them spoke. And then Matt cleared his throat. "I won't deny that I still want your help with my project," he began. As he saw her lips press together in a grim line, he hurried on. "Sarah, I'm a good filmmaker. And I honestly believe the work I'm doing on your father would make you proud of him. Let me show you what I've done in the past. If you hate it, I won't trouble you again. If you like it, we can talk about how to go on from here."

Sarah laced her fingers together tightly to keep them from trembling. Maybe she did owe Matt something. After all, he'd just saved her from a major loss in the kiln room, and she admitted that his anger last week had been provoked by hers. And while she held little hope for their personal relationship, she supposed she could still look at some of his work. She sensed that he was determined to complete this film about her father—with or without her help. She may as well get some idea of what to expect from him.

"All right," she finally conceded. "I'm not going to

promise to like it. But I'll look at whatever it is you want to show me."

Matt's face lit up. He had won a victory, even if it were a small one. At that moment, he wanted nothing more than to close the distance between them and clasp Sarah tightly in his arms. There was a lot more that he wanted from her than just her cooperation in his project. But he knew he was walking on eggshells and that he would have to be very careful. One misstep and she'd shut him out again. The only chance he had was to proceed slowly if he wanted to reach his goal.

"I know you're anxious to find out how those pieces in the kiln came out today. So why don't you come over to my place tomorrow after lunch and I'll show you some of my work."

Sarah looked at him guardedly. If he'd asked her to lunch, she would have refused. Or if he'd told her to come over in the evening, she would have been suspicious of his motives. She knew only too well how dangerous a man he could be in the moonlight. But since this would be in broad daylight, it ought to be safe enough.

"All right," she agreed.

"Then I won't bother you any more today."

Luckily Matt's warning about the kiln door really had saved the green ware. And so the only thing preying on Sarah's mind when she got ready for her visit to Matt's place was the fact that she'd be alone with him again. For that reason she took a long time selecting just the right thing to wear. No backless sun dresses or revealing shorts and T-shirts this time. She wanted to be both dignified and as covered up as the summer weather would allow. Finally, she chose a silky yellow shift with a man-tailored collar and roll-up sleeves secured by tabs. But, despite its conservative cut, it was a flattering dress, she had to admit as she inspected herself in the mirror. The bright color brought

110

out the peachy texture of her skin and the glints in her hair. And somehow the simple lines emphasized rather than hid her femininity.

For a moment she wondered if she should change. But a glance at her watch told her it was already one o'clock. And anyway, there was really nothing more appropriate in her closet.

It was the first time she'd ever been to the cottage Matt was renting. When he ushered her inside, she looked around curiously. The sunny living room, which opened onto a wide deck, was furnished with handsome and lovingly refinished pieces that had probably been garnered at country auctions and garage sales. But though their style was eclectic, they blended into a pleasant mix.

"Charming, isn't it? I was lucky to find this place," Matt commented, noting her interest.

Yes, Sarah thought dryly, he had been lucky to find such pleasant accommodations close to her. Because, of course, that had been the whole point of his renting a cottage here on the Cape. He wasn't the carefree tourist he'd pretended to be at all.

As though reading her mind, he pointed to the large television set and a Betamax in the corner of the room. "The tape I want to show you is rewound, and everything's set to go," he announced, ushering her toward the sofa opposite the television set.

As he waited politely while she sat down, she glanced at him surreptitiously. He was wearing a pair of denim cutoffs and a T-shirt. Although she'd wanted to appear businesslike, she now felt distinctly overdressed as she took the seat he'd indicated.

"Can I offer you something to drink? I have gin and tonic, or there's some iced tea in the refrigerator."

"No thank you," Sarah replied. She didn't want to accept his hospitality. That might put their relationship

111

back on too familiar a footing. All she wanted to do was see his film and go.

Shrugging, Matt switched on the set and then the Betamax. Suddenly, the soap opera which had been playing on the local station was replaced by a film title. *Walt Whitman: A Bridge to the Future.* Under the credits, a misty image of the Brooklyn Bridge loomed, and Sarah remembered that the mighty structure had been a major subject of Whitman's poetry. Using old engravings, daguerreotypes, and modern sepia-toned footage, all of which evoked the America of more than a hundred years ago, Matt's film created a visual mood that Sarah couldn't resist. The pictures were accompanied by lines from Whitman's poetry, letters, and journals, and a beautifully written narrative that wove all these elements together into a compelling portrait of a man whose work was too innovative to be appreciated by his own generation. Though she'd come to watch Matt's documentary with hypercritical eyes, Sarah couldn't help being drawn into it. She'd never understood the relationship between Whitman's poetry and his life. But Matt provided her with amazingly fresh insights into the man, and she was truly impressed.

When it was over, Sarah turned to him, unable to hide the admiration she was feeling. "It was really good!"

Matt looked almost shy, like a first-grader who was waiting for an opinion on his artwork from a favorite teacher. "Did you really like it?"

"Of course I liked it. How could I not? It was fantastic! You really have a rare talent for making a personality and an era come alive."

Matt, who had gotten up and was standing tensely by the window, relaxed visibly. "I want to do the same thing with your father. And I could do a better job because I wouldn't be working with the same limitations. So many people who knew Wallace Kiteredge and worked with him

112

are still alive. I've already interviewed some of them. But with your help, I could flesh the portrait out."

Sarah didn't really take in the end of this speech. At the first mention of her father, some of the relaxed admiration she'd been expressing so freely began to evaporate. She'd known that Matt's need for her cooperation had been the motivation for this invitation. But somehow she'd been so caught up by the artistry of the Whitman film that she'd let herself forget that. Now she vividly remembered all the feelings she'd brought into Matt's living room little more than an hour before. Then she'd been determined to simply see his film and walk out. But now she knew that wouldn't be so easy.

Weakening her resolve even further, Matt began to strengthen his argument. "Sarah, I know how protective you are of your father's privacy. But if you've looked at his work critically, you must realize that he was much more than a director of cowboy and Indian flicks."

Sarah's gaze dropped away from the intensity of Matt's green eyes. For most of her life she had simply enjoyed her father's work as straightforward entertainment. But in the past few years, when she'd caught his films on TV, she'd begun to see much more in them. At first glance, the characters might look like the usual Western stereotypes, but a closer look revealed much more. There were nuances and subtle layers of meaning in her father's productions that she was just beginning to appreciate. Perhaps Matt was right. Perhaps it would be unfair to his work to allow it to be forgotten. Maybe in trying to keep Wallace Kiteredge's name out of the public eye, she was really being selfish. But was Matt the person to do it? After the way he'd exploited their relationship, she wanted to tell herself he wasn't. But she was too honest for that. Even though he had ruined their personal relationship, he obviously had a keen sensitivity where his work was concerned.

113

What's more, he seemed to have a reverence for her father that would insure the kind of treatment he deserved.

"What do you have in mind?" she finally asked.

Matt's face lit up, and he sat down in the chair opposite, his body turned toward hers. "I can't give it to you in a neat capsule because I want to shape my plans around you. Even though we've hardly talked about your father, getting to know you has opened all sorts of possibilities I never knew existed."

Sarah's look of disbelief made him rush on before she could get up. "Give me a chance to spell it all out. Spend the day with me, Sarah. And I promise that by dinnertime we'll have worked this out together."

CHAPTER EIGHT

"I have a good dinner planned, but you're going to have to do a little work to deserve it," Matt warned.

Sarah looked up to see him emerging from the kitchen, toting two buckets with small sand shovels. Grinning engagingly, he waved one of the spades at her. "It's low tide now, the perfect time to dig clams."

She glanced down at the delicate material of the silky shift she'd worn. "But I had no intention . . . I'm not dressed—" she began.

His grin widening, Matt interrupted her protest. "I have a pair of cutoffs you can borrow. They'll be a little big on you, but women always look cute in men's clothes. They're on the chair in the bedroom," he added, gesturing toward the paneled door off the living room. "Why don't you go change while I get the rest of the stuff in the kitchen together. You can put on any of the shirts in the closet that take your fancy."

For a moment it was in Sarah's mind to refuse. She had come to Matt's house in the first place solely because he had maneuvered her into it. When she'd finally agreed to spend the rest of the day here, it was only so that she could hear his plans for a film on her father. The intimacy of changing into his clothes in his bedroom was the last thing she'd had in mind.

Sarah sighed, her feelings torn in two directions. Ever since she'd complimented him on the Whitman piece, he'd seemed so pleased. He was trying so hard to restore a friendly feeling between them, and he was smiling at her now so openly that she didn't have the heart to turn him down. In fact, the truth was that, despite everything, she wanted to spend the day with him. She had been starved for his company and was drinking in his looks and smiles as though they were a life-giving substance. That was the trouble, she told herself wryly. To destroy her most determined resistance, all Matt Lyons had to do was smile, and she melted like butter in the sun.

"Okay," she finally agreed, striving to match the lighthearted mood he was establishing. "But you'd better watch out. I've been digging clams since I could walk, and I'm probably going to make you look bad."

"I've yet to meet the lady who can one-up Mathew Lyons," he retorted impudently.

"Too true," Sarah muttered under her breath. And then waving aside his remark, she headed for the bedroom.

But once she had closed the door behind her, she looked around bemusedly. It was a small, whitewashed room with a brass double bed covered by what looked to be an old-fashioned handmade quilt. There was very little else in the way of furniture—only a captain's chair and a refinished oak chest of drawers. Yet despite its spare simplicity, everywhere there were reminders that Matt slept here. It wasn't just his clothing draped over the chair. It was the sand that clung to his running shoes on the floor at the foot of the bed, the paperback mystery novel on the windowsill, the gold cuff links on top of the bureau, and the monogrammed silver brush and comb arranged next to them. Like one in a trance, Sarah walked across the room and stood looking down at the few strands of gilded hair caught in the dark bristles. Knowing that this was foolishness, but unable to help herself, she pulled one golden thread free and let it curl across her fingers. When they'd made love, Matt's living hair had clung like this as she'd held his head to her passion-swollen breasts.

"Better hurry up or I'll go down and dig all the clams without you," she heard Matt's teasing voice say through the door.

The bittersweet expression on Sarah's fine-boned face changed to one of self-anger at her weakness. Putting down the brush, she turned abruptly away from the bureau.

It was only a matter of minutes before she'd stripped off her shift and pulled on the cutoffs. They were big on her, but Matt was narrow-hipped and, with the help of a belt she found in his closet, she was able to secure them tightly enough to keep them from slipping off. Finding a shirt she could wear was another matter. She swam in all the ones she tried and finally had to settle for a pale blue chambray. She tied the tails in a knot at her waist, but the rest hung off her shoulders ridiculously.

"I look like a scarecrow in this outfit," she complained when she came out of the bedroom.

Matt got up from the chair he'd been lounging in and looked her up and down with sparkling emerald eyes. "I think you're delectable—and sexy as hell," he added, a wicked grin curling his attractive mouth. "It's going to be a special pleasure to wear those cutoffs now that they've covered one of my favorite parts of you."

Sarah gasped at his outrageous remark and then went pink. But Matt only chuckled when he saw the bright tide of color invade her cheeks. Reaching out a hand, he stroked the heated skin delicately.

"You know how I feel about you," he told her in his deep voice. "There's no point in my pretending anything different. Your feelings may have changed toward me, but mine haven't toward you." His hand dropped away and he shrugged. "But you can relax. I promise not to make an issue of it this evening. I just want to enjoy spending

117

this time with you, okay?" Bending down easily, he hoisted the pails and shovels. "C'mon, let's go dig for our supper."

Sarah followed him out onto the redwood deck overlooking the ocean and then down the steps to the beach. In the house she had wondered how she was going to get through an evening with Matt. His nearness was so disruptive to her. She only had to look at him to feel herself yearning for his touch. But outside in the brisk air and late-afternoon sunshine, some of that sensual nervousness dissipated. When he wanted to, Matt could put a hummingbird at ease. As they squatted in the wet sand, searching for shellfish, he began to work that same magic charm on Sarah.

"This is the way life should be," he commented, watching approvingly as she flipped a sand-speckled clam into her pail. "Lie around on the beach all day and then when you get hungry, take your woman out and watch her dig up your dinner."

Sarah stiffened slightly at the term "your woman." She was not Matt Lyons's "woman," and never had been, no matter what he might think. But at the same time she found herself unwilling to destroy the pleasant feeling he had reestablished between them now by issuing a sharp reprimand. It wasn't just his lovemaking she had missed, it was being with him. "Better not get used to it," she finally retorted, making a face. "This woman is digging up just enough for *her* dinner. Your meal is up to you."

Matt looked pained. "You mean you don't intend to share?"

"I believe in equal clams for equal work," Sarah answered, looking askance at Matt's near-empty pail.

He assumed an unconvincing expression of wounded sainthood. "The clams don't like me. They're attracted to you. Wherever I dig, they burrow out of the way, but the minute you stick your shovel in the sand they hop onto it and offer up their lives."

Sarah couldn't help giggling at this ridiculous idea, and in a minute Matt's rich laughter joined hers.

Despite his claim, it wasn't long before his haul of shellfish more than matched what her pail contained. An hour later, with the lowering sun casting warm streaks of reflective light on the watery horizon, they climbed back up the beach toward Matt's deck, carrying a heavy load of the sea's delicacies.

"What now?" Sarah inquired.

Matt looked sheepish. "I don't know. I thought you'd have some suggestions."

Sarah set her heavy pail down and then, placing her hands on her hips, stared accusingly up at the blond giant next to her.

"You mean you made me dig all these clams and you don't know what to do with them?"

"You're the native Cape Codder, not me," Matt defended. "I figured you'd know how to put them in a chowder or fry them or something. But don't worry about it. Actually, I don't much care for clams myself—nasty-looking little things—so I got a steak out of the freezer just in case."

His words triggered a memory—of the first time Matt had taken her to dinner.

"Wait a minute," she accused. "You told me at that restaurant in Woods Hole that you wouldn't order lobster because you didn't like to look your dinner in the eye while it was still alive."

"So I did," Matt admitted. "But I don't think these things even have eyes. They're an entirely different kettle of fish, if you'll pardon the expression. But I'd still rather have steak."

But Sarah was not to be put off. "If you don't like clams,

119

why in the world did we just spend the afternoon filling two pails?"

Matt shrugged and shot her an endearingly boyish grin. "I just thought it would be fun—you know, digging in the sand together like a couple of kids. I was hoping that seeing what a child I am at heart might appeal to your maternal instincts."

Sarah was outraged. "Matt Lyons, now that we've dug those clams, we're going to eat them. But first they have to be cleaned."

Matt looked appalled. "Cleaned? Yuk!"

Sarah shook her head in mock despair. "They should be put in clean water for a hour or so. We'll rinse them off and put them in a pail. And while they're soaking, you can tell me about your ideas. I thought that was the whole purpose of this day, anyhow."

Matt looked down into Sarah's flushed features with a faint, rueful smile. "Yes, I want to tell you my ideas. But my ideas aren't just about your father," he murmured.

Sarah's dark eyebrows drew together, and she averted her face from his questioning gaze. "You promised you wouldn't do this," she accused in a smothered voice. "I'm willing to listen to what you have to say about your project, but nothing else. If you start to talk about us, I'm leaving."

The silence tautened for a moment, and then Matt sighed. "Okay, I'm sorry. We'll rinse the clams and then talk. Do you want to change back into your dress?"

Sarah shook her head. "No," she said, pointing down into her bucket. "When it comes time to shuck off those shells I might as well not be wearing my good clothes."

Matt grinned, and some of the good-natured ease he'd shown earlier came back into his face. "You really meant it about eating those things?"

Sarah made an exasperated noise in her throat. "I really

120

meant it. Now, if we want to eat before midnight, we'd better get going on this."

Half an hour later, she was sitting comfortably in a webbed lounge chair on Matt's deck. As Sarah sipped at the tall, cool gin and tonic he'd just mixed for her, she admired the view. She loved the ocean and once again marveled at how different it could look, depending on the weather and the vantage point. From the distant height of her bedroom window it spread out like a blue, frothy carpet, challenging in its vastness. But from Matt's deck it was closer and friendlier somehow. Suddenly drowsy from the sun and the effect of the drink she was sipping, Sarah closed her eyes and let the soothing sound of the waves wash through her system like a balm.

"Hey, don't go to sleep on me." Matt chuckled.

Sarah's eyes snapped open, and she saw him emerging from the sliding glass doors clutching a sheaf of papers. Struggling to throw off her lethargy, she asked, "What are those?"

"Notes on my project," he explained, spreading them out on the round patio table and drawing up a chair.

"Do you work at home in New York, too?" Sarah asked, suddenly curious about his real life.

Matt nodded. "I'm like you in that. I like having my studio and living quarters right next to each other. But we were going to discuss my ideas for the film, remember?"

Sarah nodded and pushed her own chair toward the table. "Okay. Fire away."

Picking up the first sheet, Matt began to explain his concepts for the film. At first Sarah was confused by the barrage of ideas, facts, and figures he shot at her. But gradually, as his notions began to take shape in her mind, some of his enthusiasm about the film began to affect her. And he *was* enthusiastic, she mused, studying his mobile features and sparkling eyes from under her lashes. He was as excited about, and absorbed in, his own work as she so often was about hers. Vividly, she recalled the feverish, trancelike afternoon of creativity in which her ideas for *Dream Woman* had finally taken shape. In that mood, nothing short of a cyclone could have stopped her from completing her self-appointed task. Matt was probably the same way about his films, she realized with sudden insight. It was because of his dedication to his creative work that he had used his relationship with her. Though the knowledge still hurt, she could, as an artist, begin to understand the powerful forces that had motivated him.

Matt's hands were gesturing expressively, framing a picture in the air. "Can't you just see how effective that opening shot is going to be?" he demanded.

Smiling indulgently, Sarah glanced at her watch and then set down her empty glass. "Maybe I can and maybe I can't. You can explain it to me some more while we're doing something about dinner."

Matt's face fell ludicrously. "Do you mean you're going to make me shuck those things?"

Sarah shook her head so that her dark hair swung around her shoulders in a loose curtain. "Nope. While you've been telling me some of your creative ideas, I've been having a few of my own. We're going to have a clambake. Now, do you have a shovel so we can dig a pit? Or am I going to have to get one from my place?"

It was not until much later that evening, long after the sun had set and the stars were twinkling in the black velvet canopy above the beach, that Sarah and Matt finally finished their impromptu dinner. Despite Matt's reservations, when the clams had been placed on preheated rocks, covered with seaweed and a piece of canvas, and then allowed to steam open, they were delicious. To go with the main course, Matt produced grilled corn, a salad, and a bottle of Chablis.

"To the loveliest clambaker on Cape Cod," he murmured as he refilled Sarah's glass with the last of the white wine. "You've made a convert out of me. From now on I'll be out with my spade and shovel all the time, digging away in the sand in hopes a gorgeous woman will emerge and cook a fabulous dinner for me."

In playful annoyance, Sarah flicked some wine at him from her brimming glass. "You're just lazy. You probably take stuff out of your freezer all the time and never bother to make anything fresh."

Matt, who'd been stretched out on the blanket in front of the glowing fire pit, rolled toward her so that his eyes met hers at close range. "That's true. But you could change my ways. You could cook for me all the time."

Sarah was suddenly uncomfortable. They were getting onto dangerous ground again. All afternoon the undercurrent of sensuality between them had plagued her. And she knew that unless she did something about it, helping Matt with his project, as she now wanted to do, would be impossible. "I'm not the domestic type. I'm not interested in cooking all the time."

"You wouldn't have to," Matt quickly countered. "If you told me what to buy and how to fix it, I'd do the cooking. I just want to spend time with you," he added, his eyes remaining on hers. He had propped his elbow on the blanket, and his firm chin was resting in his cupped palm. For what seemed like a long time, he regarded Sarah where she lay, her own head on a folded blanket that made a makeshift pillow.

Matt's eyes seemed to pierce her through the firelit shadows, and once again she felt the tug of his magnetism. She knew from the simmering heat in his eyes what he was thinking. He wanted to make love to her. And right now she wanted it, too. There was no point in lying to herself about that. But Sarah wasn't going to allow it to happen. Despite all her precautions, she'd let down her guard today and enjoyed the pleasure of being with him. But beyond that, she just wasn't ready to renew their intimacy. There were too many risks, too many uncertainties.

"I've missed you," he told her, his deep voice ringing with sincerity. And then suddenly, he was closer yet, his face only inches from hers and his hand reaching out to touch her shoulder. "I kept looking over at your house, wanting to catch a glimpse of you. And I watched the beach. It hurt me when you kicked the messages I left for you into smithereens." He smiled ruefully, and Sarah regretted what she'd done. She'd been reacting like an angry child.

"I'm sorry," she told him.

He nodded. "But then when you couldn't throw Eustace away, that gave me hope."

Sarah stiffened. "Hope for what?"

Matt's hand reached out to softly stroke her shoulder. "Hope that you wouldn't be able to throw me away, either." His face began to bend toward hers, and she knew that in a moment their lips would be touching. It horrified her to realize how desperately she wanted that kiss. Her whole being seemed to dissolve with weakness. And it wasn't just his kiss that she wanted. Once his mouth was on her lips, her arms would be stealing about his shoulders, drawing him down so their bodies could intertwine.

As Sarah realized the depths of her vulnerability, a dart of pure panic pierced her, and she averted her face from his. She simply could not allow this man to disarm her so completely. Maybe his motives were understandable. But it was an undeniable fact that he had deceived her. And who knew what his attitude would be when his film was finally complete?

"Oh, Sarah, please don't turn away from me," Matt crooned.

But Sarah only shook her head and clenched her lower lip between her teeth to keep it from trembling. "I have to," she finally managed. "Listen, Matt, I'm willing to help you, but only under certain conditions."

He sighed and drew back. "What conditions?"

Sarah turned and faced him squarely. "That our relationship is strictly professional, that there be nothing physical between us, and that you don't try to pressure me into sleeping with you."

Matt's voice was rough. "Pressure. You know damn well I wasn't pressuring you."

Sarah sighed. "Okay. I wanted you, too. But you know what I'm saying. I'll help you, but I'll not fall into bed with you again. Do you understand?"

Matt sat up and raked his hand through his tumbled blond locks. "Yes, I understand."

"And do you agree to my conditions?" Sarah persisted.

Matt's chin had a rebellious cast to it, but he nodded. "Yes, I agree."

Sarah took a deep breath. "All right, then, I'll help you gather material for your film. We can start tomorrow if you like."

As Sarah packed a picnic lunch the next day, she wondered once again about her decision. While her hands busily mixed tuna fish salad and sliced cucumbers, her mind was on the afternoon. She would be taking Matt to some of the special places she remembered visiting with her father—starting with the old lighthouse where they'd scavenged the round stones that now lined the front flower beds. The itinerary she'd planned would keep them busy for the next few days. And then there were the old family albums she'd dug out of the attic.

They were full of slightly yellowed pictures that could have been shot by the publicity department of Global Studios. Besides the family shots, those pictures showed her parents together, looking happy and contented. No one would guess from those smiling faces that her father's warmest feelings were for another woman and not for his strikingly beautiful, blond, blue-eyed wife.

As she spread mayonnaise on cracked wheat bread, Sarah remembered one photo in particular. It was of a picnic down on the beach in front of their house. Her father was feeding her mother a sandwich and laughing into her flushed face. Actually, Patricia Kiteredge had rarely looked so animated as that picture showed her. Sarah remembered her as a quiet, home-loving woman, who'd never been able to adapt to the fast life in Hollywood or the money her father had made. Even when they'd been able to afford the best interior decorator, she'd spent hours making her own slipcovers.

"Get up from that damn sewing machine and come sailing with me!" Wallace Kiteredge had bellowed one afternoon. But his wife had refused, just as she'd refused to go to any of the studio parties, to attend any of the premieres, and finally even to live in Hollywood at all. After three years in what she referred to as "that artificial environment," she'd moved herself and her daughters back to Cape Cod, and her husband had been forced to commute from the west coast to see his family. Now that Sarah had gotten over the shock after learning the truth, she realized that perhaps it wasn't so surprising to learn that he'd found another woman.

But Sarah wasn't going to tell Matt about any of that. It wasn't what she wanted the public to know about her father. And it wouldn't be fair to her mother's memory, either.

Her mother and father had been high school sweethearts, Sarah knew. And now she guessed they had married too young, without really understanding each other's goals and needs. Patricia had been assuming she'd be living the same sort of low-key life she'd always known on Cape Cod. And she hadn't understood why her young husband had refused to go into his father's lumber business in order to pursue the uncertainty of life as a filmmaker. At first she'd lived at home with her parents, hoping that her husband would give up the crazy idea. But when he'd succeeded in establishing himself in Hollywood, that had eventually driven more of a wedge into their relationship. Sarah knew that her mother hadn't understood her father's artistic aspirations. She couldn't have appreciated what he was really striving for in his films. And he, in turn, had little patience for the conservative woman who refused to make herself part of his life.

Through it all, however, Wallace Kiteredge had never abandoned his family. Even though his visits were infrequent, he remained close to Sarah and Bev. And he must have felt something for his marriage, too, Sarah told herself now, because he'd never tried to end it.

So, the picture she wanted Matt to present in his film wasn't entirely a false one, Sarah assured herself. It would remain true to her father's spirit, if not to the letter of his life.

After tucking the last sandwich into its clear plastic bag, Sarah rummaged under the counter for the thermos jug and began to fill it with lemonade. By the time Matt arrived twenty minutes later, everything was neatly packed and ready to go.

They spent the day visiting all of Wallace Kiteredge's boyhood haunts. Sarah took Matt down to the secluded harbor where her father had kept a small sailboat as a youngster, and they picnicked on the end of one of its worn docks.

"Dad was always an avid sailor," Sarah had explained, looking out over the sun-brightened water and remembering the last time she'd seen him before the accident.

Matt had nodded sympathetically. "That might be a good way to start my film," he commented. "It could begin with shots of a sloop turning into the wind."

Sarah shivered. She'd hated to picture the way her par-

127

ents had died, but she had to acknowledge that the image Matt suggested would be a powerful one.

"It's ironic that your parents were together in that boating accident," he commented, giving her a curious look.

Sarah was instantly defensive. "Why do you say that?"

"Well, you and your mother lived here while he spent most of his time on the west coast, didn't he?"

"But he came back to see us all the time," Sarah insisted, and then quickly changed the subject.

Over the next few days Matt and Sarah spent almost all their time together. While Matt filmed with his portable video camera balanced on his shoulder, Sarah led him to every nook and cranny of the area where Wallace Kiteredge had grown up. They visited the lighthouse Sarah remembered so well, toured the schools he'd gone to, and followed the route he'd taken as a paperboy.

Being with Matt this way and reliving her father's past was a strange experience for Sarah. As they discussed Wallace Kiteredge, she was amazed at Matt's insights and was forced to rethink some of her preconceived notions.

"Do you realize that even though your father made Westerns, all of his films are permeated with water imagery," Matt asked one afternoon. They were lazing on her father's rowboat, looking inland on a stretch of shoreline he must have seen many times.

"What do you mean?" Sarah questioned.

Matt waved an encompassing hand at the shore. "Take that scene in *Prairie Schooners* where the wagon trains are setting out across the desert. The desert might as well be the ocean, and the whole mood of it is very similar to what we're experiencing now. And then there's that marvelous set piece where Buck Fielding crosses the Rio Grande. Now that I've seen where your father grew up, I know what inspired him."

For a moment Sarah could only stare bemusedly. He

was right, she realized. Though she'd known and loved her father for years, Matt was explaining things to her she'd never really seen or understood. And all at once she had the feeling that in bringing Matt and her father together this way, she was somehow fusing the past and the present. For if her father had been the most important man in her past, Matt had that role now. Though she'd tried to tell herself it wasn't true, that was becoming impossible to deny. These last few days had shown her that despite everything, she still wanted him. When they'd first started this pilgrimage, she'd told herself that it would be strictly a businesslike arrangement. But even then she'd known that was absurd. She couldn't be near Matt and not remember his caress. She couldn't walk beside him without hoping that their bodies might accidentally touch. And she couldn't lie here in this boat with him and not want to reach out and run her hand along his strong, bronzed arm the way she had the first evening before they'd made love.

Pensively, Sarah stole a glance up at Matt's profile from under lowered lashes. He was resting easily on the oars and looking out over the water. But as if he sensed what was going on in her mind, he turned and met her eyes. His green gaze seemed to lock with hers and then penetrate to her very soul. Slowly his hand reached out and touched her sun-warmed cheek. Sarah could only look at him wordlessly, her heart in her eyes as his hand stroked gently down the side of her face and then rested lightly on her throat where a tiny pulse surged up and began to throb in response.

He had kept his side of their bargain. It had been days since he had touched her with this kind of familiarity. And though the contact was the lightest of feather brushes, she could feel her body responding as though he were actually holding her in his arms. The skin of her neck and cheeks flushed at the realization and, as he watched the warm tide that brought a glow of color to her face, his own green gaze intensified. And then his gaze was drawn lower. She knew he was looking at the rounded outline of her breasts under her lilac T-shirt. The flush on her face and neck were not the only betrayal of her body's sensual stirrings. At the thought of making love with Matt, her nipples had tautened. And now she knew that he was seeing them strain toward him through the clinging knit fabric.

She saw his knuckles whiten as his hands closed around the oars. A flush that matched hers began to creep into his lean cheeks, and the emerald green of his eyes darkened a shade.

"Sarah," he murmured, and she knew it was a question. But the words she wanted to say stuck in her throat. Her response to him must be obvious. But how could she admit out loud that she wanted him, that she was longing for him. That seemed impossible after she'd made such a point of putting him off.

"Sarah," he repeated, his gaze holding hers with a searing intensity. "You know I'm leaving for New York tomorrow to put the film together. Tonight will be my last night on the Cape." He paused, letting his meaning become clear. And then added, "Will you stay with me?"

Time seemed to hang suspended while Sarah deliberated her answer. She was in love with Matt. She had to admit that now. With all her heart and soul she wanted to stay with him. But he had come right out and told her he was leaving tomorrow. What did that mean? Was it a way of letting her know this would be their last time together? To keep from being hurt, she had told herself from the beginning that her relationship with Matt could only end one way. But now that she was looking at that brick wall, she didn't have the courage to face it—or to ask him if that was what it really meant. All she knew now was that this might be her last chance to hold the man she loved in her arms. And whatever the future, she wanted tonight.

"Yes," she finally whispered. And as Matt turned to row them back to shore, they both knew that she'd agreed to more than just an evening in his company.

CHAPTER NINE

Both Sarah and Matt knew that they had come to an unspoken agreement in the boat—about tonight, at any rate. There was no more need for the silent feinting and parrying of the sexual duel that had taken up so much of their energy during the last few days.

There was no need to shrink away from Matt's hand as he reached out to help her step from the boat up onto the weathered dock. Having made her decision, Sarah was free to savor the promise of the warm contact and to imagine how those sensitive fingers entwined with hers would feel on her body later on tonight. And when she looked up into Matt's face after he'd secured the small dory, she knew he was thinking the same thing. The shared knowledge made them both smile into each other's eyes. And yet for Sarah there was a bittersweet flavor hovering around the edges of her happiness. She refused, though, to let it spoil things. She was determined to gather in what happiness with Matt might be left to her. If she were living in a fantasy world, so be it.

Hand in hand they strolled to the sandy shoulder of the road where Matt had parked his car. And after he'd settled her on the passenger seat, his hand lingered on her arm before he went around to open his own door.

"What shall we make for dinner tonight?" he questioned, making a U-turn on the narrow blacktop and heading back toward town.

Sarah shook her head. Food had been the last thing on her mind this afternoon.

"Well, those steaks we didn't eat the other night are still in the freezer. Why don't I bring them over and grill them."

"Let's stop at a farm stand for corn and tomatoes, then," Sarah suggested. "I've already got lettuce and cucumbers in my refrigerator."

Matt nodded his agreement. And while his sports car sped along the deserted country road, Sarah leaned back to enjoy the warm air from the open window fanning her cheeks and the soft lash of her own hair against her neck as the wind whipped loose strands around.

The man next to her slanted a caressing glance in her direction. "You look so lovely with your hair caught in the breeze that way," he murmured.

Self-consciously, Sarah put up a hand to straighten her unruly locks. But Matt reached over and stopped her. "Don't," he growled softly. "I like to see you that way. It reminds me how you'll look tonight when we make love."

Suddenly Sarah was unable to meet his gaze. But his bold remark had triggered a series of wanton images in her own imagination. Her whole body was suddenly suffused with a warm glow. It seemed to start in her abdomen and spread upward to her breasts and downward through her legs as well. And then she felt a more intense heat as Matt's hand left the steering wheel to stroke the soft skin of her thigh under the cuff of her shorts.

"Like silk," he whispered huskily.

Sarah shivered in reaction but made no attempt to remove the bronzed palm resting against her skin. She waited, wondering if his invading hand would explore further. Sighing with pleasure, she leaned her head back against his shoulder. But the tantalizing hand remained still on her thigh.

"I promised you dinner," Matt muttered ruefully. "But

133

if I do what I want to do now, we'll either end up wrapped around a tree or I'll have to stop the car and drag you into the woods."

Gently he squeezed her thigh and then replaced his hand on the steering wheel.

With a sigh, Sarah started to move away. But his arm swung around her shoulders to pull her back against him. "I was recommending caution, not total deprivation." He chuckled.

A few minutes later they stopped at a roadside stand to pick up the vegetables for dinner. And then Matt dropped Sarah off at her house. "I'll be around at six with two beautiful steaks," he promised.

Sarah glanced at her watch. She had two hours to get ready for what promised to be a very special evening. After shucking the corn and slicing the tomatoes, she prepared the salad she'd promised Matt and then covered it with a wet towel so that the greens would remain crisp. But while she worked over the food, her mind was on more intimate preparations. A scented bath would be the first step. And then she'd have to pick something flattering and unique to wear. There were a number of dramatic outfits in her closet that she usually ignored. Though they'd been appropriate when she'd lived in Hollywood, they were far too sexy for the quiet life she usually led on the Cape. But tonight she wasn't going to be cautious. She was going to be as alluring as possible.

As she relaxed in the lilac-scented water of her old-fashioned claw-footed tub, she suddenly knew which of her designer outfits would be exactly right for the mood she wanted to set tonight: her floor-length hostess gown of misty blue with the tight halter top and the long flowing skirt.

A half hour later, standing before the long mirror, Sarah was more than satisfied with the effect she had created. As she had known it would, the dress showed off her full breasts and revealed a creamy expanse of naked back whenever she turned. And as her skirt swirled with her every movement, it flirted tantalizingly with the long, elegant line of her legs. It was obvious that the dress was not made to wear with a bra. But only Sarah knew, as she twisted and turned, examining her image, how brazen she really was tonight. At the last moment, she'd decided to wear no panties under that seductively swirling skirt.

When she had slipped into delicate silver sandals and pinned her long hair back from her face with silver combs, she was ready to go down and set the table.

Just as she'd put a lot of thought into her outfit, she'd also been considering the effect she wanted to create in the dining room. It had been a long time since she'd used her grandmother's delicate French china and hand-chased silver. For this evening with Matt, however, they seemed right. But when she'd arranged two place settings on a white lace cloth, the table still missed something. It was only when she'd added a crystal vase with fragrant roses from the garden and two silver candlesticks with long white tapers that she was satisfied.

She was just standing back to admire the effect she'd created when there was a tap at the door. It was Matt. He, too, must have considered this occasion very special. Instead of his usual casual attire, he was wearing classic white summer trousers and a fitted European-style jacket with thin dark stripes. Under the jacket, a fog-gray silk shirt was opened at the collar, revealing the strong, erect line of his throat.

In addition to the steaks, he was carrying a bottle of sparkling burgundy.

When she opened the door, he just stood there looking at her for a moment, taking in the silver-and-blue effect of her as she stood there, slim and graceful, in her long gown. "Breathtaking," he finally said. "You should always dress this way."

Sarah laughed. "I could say the same for you. You look pretty fantastic, too. But we'd make an odd-looking pair jogging like this on the beach tomorrow morning."

Matt's eyes seemed to heat, and she knew what he was thinking. By tomorrow morning the stylish clothes they both wore would probably be in a heap on her bedroom floor.

"I could skip dinner without too much pain right now, Sarah," he said huskily, stepping into the front hall and putting the bottle of burgundy down on the sideboard.

"Oh, no, you don't!" Sarah countered with a mischievous grin. "I've spent too much time getting ready for this."

Ushering him into the living room, she pointed through the arch at the elegantly set table.

Matt whistled through his teeth. "I see what you mean. I'm impressed. And it will be a lovely setting in which to contemplate you as we eat."

Sarah had been right. The romantic atmosphere she had created as a setting for their dinner was the perfect beginning to the pleasures of the evening. As they ate, they glanced at each other frequently through the soft halo of the candles flickering in the center of the table. And though their conversation was relaxed, there was a fine silken filament of desire spinning its silvery web between them. It shielded them from the outside world and drew their souls together. So that when dinner was finished and they sipped the last ruby drops of their wine, they were almost as one in their hunger for each other.

"Do you know that in the candlelight, with your hair around your shoulders, you look like a painting?" Matt asked, setting down his glass and leaning forward in his chair.

"I hope not one of Picasso's mixed-up ladies," Sarah returned playfully. "You know, the ones with their noses and ears all in the same spot."

But Matt's expression as he shook his fair head remained serious. "Everything you've got is in exactly the right place. No, I was thinking of one of those Renaissance Aphrodites. To me you're as beautiful as a goddess of love rising from the ocean, Sarah. In fact, that's the way I first saw you, running beside the sea with a joyful expression on your face, your hair streaming out in a cloud behind you."

Sarah's gaze dropped shyly from his, and she looked down into her wineglass. "It makes me feel good to run. But I don't usually wear my hair loose. Normally, it's in braids."

Matt reached over and took a strand of the rich, dark stuff between his fingers. "It's loose now. It's the way I like it—the way I've been thinking of it all afternoon."

Sarah looked up, and her eyes met the dark green depths of his with a small shock. "You've been thinking of it all afternoon?"

"I've been thinking of you," Matt corrected. "Since I drove away from your house, you've never left my mind. You were in my thoughts when I parked my car in the drive, when I opened the door and walked into my living room. Even when I showered, I imagined you there with me under the water."

Sarah stared at him in fascination, unconsciously running a hand along the bare length of her opposite arm. "What did we do?" she asked huskily.

Matt laced his long fingers together on the tablecloth. "I pictured myself washing your back and shoulders. You don't know how beautiful your naked back is, but it takes my breath away to think of it. I wondered how it would be to soap your breasts and then hold them in my hands while the water rinsed us off."

"Matt!" Sarah protested, feeling herself go pink as she began to picture the scene he described.

"I wanted to press you close to my body and whisper naughty things in your ear," he continued.

Suddenly unable to sit still, she rose from her chair and walked through the wide arch that opened onto the living room. The light in there was subdued also. Candles flickered on two side tables, bathing the elegantly furnished room in a rich glow. But as Sarah stood with her hands resting on the back of a velvet wing chair, she was hardly aware of her surroundings. She was trembling slightly as she thought of the desire glowing in Matt's eyes when he looked at her across the table. And then she heard the soft tread of his feet on the carpet directly behind her. He had followed her into the room. Putting his hands on her bare shoulders, he gently turned her toward him and looked caressingly down into her face. "You're beautiful in that dress," he told her in a deep voice. "But you're even more beautiful the way I imagined you this afternoon. It's been driving me crazy, Sarah. Let me make love to you, the way I pictured it."

As his hands lightly stroked her shoulders, she could only gaze up into his face mutely. She wanted his touch with a fierce hunger. At the thought of his hands on her flesh, she seemed to ache all over with unsatisfied longing.

Wordlessly, he touched his lips to her forehead, her eyebrows, and then her eyelids. The light caresses were unbearably stimulating, and Sarah shivered as his mouth moved down the line of her throat and then came to rest in the vee of her neckline where his tongue darted in and out teasingly. She made no protest when he undid the halter top of her dress and slipped it down to her waist.

As the candlelight played over Sarah's ivory curves, so did Matt's hungry scrutiny. One of his hands went to the small of her back and he gently, but firmly, arched her toward him so that her full breasts were accessible to his lips. And then his head bent and he circled each pink tip with his tongue, seeming to savor their delicate taste and texture. As his lips played deliciously over her passion-sensitized breasts, Sarah leaned against the velvet chair and let her head fall back, lost to the sensations that were rippling through her. In a brief flash of insight, it occurred to her that the ecstatic expression on her face must be very like that of *Dream Woman*'s. But as Matt's lips and hands began to move softly down her torso, she was not capable of holding any coherent thought for long. She could only wait with heady anticipation for what her lover might do next.

"In my imagination," he told her in a thickened voice, "I didn't just wash your breasts. I soaped your stomach and then your thighs."

Suddenly Sarah realized that he was kneeling before her, his hands curved around her buttocks through the soft material of her gown. "I washed every bit of you," he added as his lips dropped a line of kisses along the bare flesh of her slender waist where the top part of her gown was folded down.

"Oh, Matt," Sarah breathed. Her voice seemed to catch in her throat, making her inarticulate. All she could do was twine her fingers in the heavy gold of his hair. One of his hands had moved down the length of her silken gown to her sandaled feet. Now he slipped his hand under the silver-shot fabric of her full skirt, and she felt his warm fingers encircle her ankle. "Every beautiful bit of you," he repeated as his hand began to slide slowly up the line of her leg. "Your calves, your lovely, smooth knees." His exploring fingers paused to stroke a sensual pattern around and behind that part of her leg, and then once more they quested upward inch by tantalizing inch. "I love your thighs, Sarah. They're so firm and smooth. In my imagination this afternoon I seemed to spend hours adoring your thighs."

Sarah gasped at his boldness, hotly aware that she wore no panties under her full skirt. The part of her that most longed for his touch was only inches from his grasp. But while one of Matt's hands still held and stroked her buttocks through the fabric of her dress, the other loitered on the flesh of her thigh, caressing and fondling. It wasn't until Sarah's legs had begun to tremble and she feared she could no longer hold herself up on them that Matt's fingers began once more to track a fiery path upward.

"How wonderfully satisfying it is to have you in my arms like this, instead of just imagining how it would be," he murmured. Pressing her closer, he rubbed his lips lightly along the bare flesh of her midriff and then dipped lower to nuzzle the indentation of her navel. At the same time, he slid his hand up the last soft inch of her inner thigh. It was then that he realized there was no barrier between his hand and her most intimate secrets. He drew back to stare up at her flushed features with eyes of fiery emerald. "My God, Sarah," he whispered huskily. "You're not wearing anything under this skirt."

While he spoke, his hand continued to caress her. Sarah was already aglow with the heat his sensuous explorations had inspired. Now that she felt Matt's fingers stroking a delicate, knowing pattern on her most sensitive feminine parts, she shuddered with excitement. Her hands clutched his shoulders convulsively. "Oh, Matt," she warned. "If you don't stop . . ."

But Matt knew exactly what he was doing. And in the next instant Sarah was beyond words. Shudders of electric excitement thrilled through her and then seemed to burst into showers of delicious sparks. She sagged against him, wedged between his body and the wing chair. For a moment Matt held her, burying his face in the material of her skirt that covered the softness between her thighs. And then he stood and swept her limp body into his arms. Passionately, he kissed the tip of each bare breast, and then he looked into her heavy-lidded eyes.

"Do you know what touching you like this has done to

me?" But he didn't wait for her answer. Instead, he turned and strode toward the staircase in the hall. "I'm going to carry you upstairs to bed and show you what it's done to me," he whispered gruffly into her ear.

When Sarah awoke the next morning, Matt was propped up on his elbow beside her, looking into her face with an amused smile on his face. He was holding a strand of her hair between his fingers, and she knew that he'd been stroking her cheek with it. She was also aware that his long, hard body was touching her at several points and that they were both naked under the blue-flowered sheet covering them.

"You're beautiful when you're asleep, and I almost couldn't bear to wake you up," he commented, playfully twirling the strand of hair around in his fingers. "But I do have to leave for New York soon, and I wanted us to have breakfast together."

Despite the warmth of Matt's body enfolding hers, the casually spoken words made Sarah suddenly feel cold. She'd known, of course, that Matt would be leaving today. In fact, that was what had made her finally admit that she wanted him back in her bed again. But what next?

The question hovered on the edge of her lips. The way to find out what was in Matt's mind was to ask him. But suppose she asked and he told her that this was the end of their affair? She knew she just couldn't stand hearing that now.

Matt's expression was as unclouded as that of a Boy Scout going off to camp. If he were simply planning to climb out of her bed and leave in a couple of hours, he obviously had no real regrets. But it was an heroic effort for Sarah to match his sunny smile.

"How about letting me fix breakfast?" he offered. "Last time when you did it, things didn't turn out so well."

Sarah's expression darkened, but Matt chose not to

notice. "Some juice, scrambled eggs, and a hot cup of coffee are just what you need," he promised, climbing quickly out of bed.

As he stood with his back to her, stretching luxuriously so that the muscles in his broad back and legs rippled, Sarah's couldn't stop her gaze from roaming hungrily over his tall, narrow-hipped body. He was magnificent, she told herself once more. And she marveled again that a man who could so obviously have any woman he chose had wanted *her* for a lover. Why couldn't she simply have kept it on that level? she asked herself. Why had she let herself fall in love with him?

And what did she mean to him? she wondered once more. She knew he cared for her. Their lovemaking last night had been explosively passionate and infinitely satisfying. He couldn't have made love to her the way he'd done last night and not cared. But she was a grown woman who'd lived long enough to know that he had his own life apart from her. For him this had probably been just a romantic interlude, one of many that a man like him would enjoy. And that he showed no signs of regret now that he was leaving her only confirmed that fact. The best thing she could do was let him go gracefully. A moment ago she'd felt angry and betrayed when he'd casually reminded her of that other life. But that wasn't being fair, she told herself. What would it accomplish to let him see how angry and hurt she was at the idea of his going? That would only ruin their last moments together and spoil the memory of what they had shared. Last night had been beautiful. She would let it stay that way, she vowed.

Matt had pulled on his slacks. "Why don't you relax in bed, my dear, and your humble servant will bring breakfast up on a tray—that is, if he can have the pleasure of sharing it with you."

Sarah forced herself to return Matt's sunny smile with

a cheerful one of her own. "If you're trying to make me feel spoiled, you're succeeding."

"I enjoy spoiling you," Matt assured her on his way out.

As Sarah lay in bed, gathering her strength to face the end of the summer idyll that had meant so much to her, she could hear Matt downstairs in the kitchen rattling pans. She supposed, like most male cooks, he would leave a mess. But that was the least of her concerns right now.

Twenty minutes later, he reappeared at the bedroom door carrying one of her best silver trays. Besides the eggs, juice, and coffee he'd promised, it bore a plate of golden, buttered toast and a small cut glass vase with one of the pink roses from last night's table setting.

"That looks wonderful," Sarah told him sincerely. And it did, too. She hadn't realized before that she was hungry, but the sight of Matt's offering was making her stomach growl. But as she sat up in bed and Matt's eyes focused on her breasts, she realized she was still naked. "I'd better put on my dressing gown," Sarah murmured, sinking back down under the sheets.

"If you must, my love." Matt chuckled. "But don't expect me to be a gentleman and look the other way. I intend to enjoy our last morning together to the fullest."

The reminder was like the touch of a cold hand. Without another word Sarah slipped out of bed and went to the closet to pull on her eyelet robe. Matt's gaze followed her every move, and when she had pulled the ties tight around her waist and turned back to him, his eyes were glowing with a banked green fire.

Repressing the uncomfortable mixture of emotions she felt, Sarah plumped up the bed pillows and straightened the covers. When she'd arranged herself in the bed once more, Matt placed the tray on her lap and then sat down beside her. He hadn't yet bothered to put on a shirt, and Sarah's gaze was momentarily caught by the way the golden hairs on his broad chest glinted in the morning sunlight.

His hand reached over to the tray and, ceremoniously, he poured them each a richly aromatic cup of coffee. And then he snagged a wedge of toast from the plate and began to munch on it. Sarah started in on her eggs, but as she ate she was conscious of his eyes on her. For several minutes they continued their breakfast in silence. And then Matt's deep voice broke the quiet.

"I love the way you look in the morning, Sarah."

She shot him a brief look and laughed self-consciously. "You mean with no makeup and my hair in a tangle?"

But Matt nodded seriously. "Yes, to me you're as beautiful now as you were when you were all dressed up. I love your hair in a tangle." He reached out a finger and touched her face almost reverently. "I love your nose," he declared, giving it a tender kiss. "I love your ear." His tongue circled the pink outside rim. "I love your mouth." His thumb touched itself gently to her lips. "I love your throat," he whispered as his lips slid down the length of her neck to the hollow where her pulse throbbed.

Carefully, Sarah lay her fork down on the tray. Her fingers were trembling and, under the thin covering of her robe, all of her body was coming alive under Matt's touch. Desperately she wanted him to make love to her again, and yet, how could she allow him to when the moment he would leave her was so close? It would be more pain than she could bear.

Matt's lips slid now to her collarbone and then downward to the vee between her breasts where the robe closed. And she could feel her nipples begin to ache with response. "And there are many more things about you that I love," he murmured. "In fact, I love all of you."

He was trying to arouse her passion with those words. And he was succeeding. She wanted him now more than she'd ever wanted him before. Her whole body seemed to

144

throb with that unsatisfied longing. But at the same time she was cut by the cruelty of his using words she wanted so much to believe. And yet she had focused her mind so squarely on the fact that their relationship was ending that she simply couldn't believe him.

Defensively, she pushed his head away and picked up her coffee cup to take a sip. "I'll bet you say that to all the naked ladies you wake up with in the morning," she quipped, using all her strength to make her voice light and carefree.

"No, actually, I don't," Matt informed her, a frown creasing the skin between his dark eyebrows. "In fact, I've never said it to anyone before." Getting up abruptly from the bed, he turned and stared out the window for a moment, his hands on his hips as she had seen him stand so many times before. Only instead of the relaxation the pose usually denoted, now his body looked tense.

Had she been too quick with her flippant observation? Sarah wondered. But in the next second, Matt had turned back to her, his smile back in place. "Well, I guess we'd better finish up. I've got to be back in New York this evening, you know. If you're done with that tray, I'll take it down."

Here was the moment Sarah had been steeling herself for, and silently dreading. But if she could just get through the next ten minutes without making a fool of herself, she would have won some sort of small victory, at least in her own mind if not in Matt's estimation.

"Of course," she murmured, setting down the coffee cup and moving the tray so that she could swing her legs off the bed and get up. "It looks like you have perfect driving weather, at any rate," she added, sweeping an encompassing hand toward the window.

Matt nodded, turning to pick up his shirt from the floor where he had discarded it with such passion-driven negligence only the night before. Noticing with a sinking feeling that his eyes seemed to be avoiding hers, she watched him button it up and then look for his shoes and jacket. After donning shoes and socks, he stood up and slung the jacket carelessly over his shoulder. "Well, I guess this is good-bye, then," he offered.

"Yes," she managed, and then added, "take care on the way back." It was an effort to force the words around the lump in her throat. But she was determined she wasn't going to let Matt Lyons see just how much his leavetaking was affecting her.

"There's no need to come down with me," he assured her. "You might even want to go back to bed. After all, you didn't get much sleep last night." He might have meant the words callously. But for her the reprieve was merciful. If she'd had to go downstairs and see him out the door, she might not have been able to maintain the dispassionate facade she had so far successfully affected.

Matt turned and looked at her for a long moment, his features absolutely expressionless. "Good-bye, Sarah," he finally said, leaning down to brush his lips briefly over her forehead. "When you come down to New York for that show of yours, maybe you'll want to stop by my studio and see the film. It should be finished by then."

Sarah blinked. She'd been concentrating so hard on the pain of this farewell that she'd forgotten all about the damn film. But of course that had been the reason why he'd come here in the first place. Her mouth tightened slightly and she stiffened her back. "I'll try to make the time," she told him evenly.

Matt didn't answer. Instead he merely nodded and turned away. The next moment he had disappeared out the door of her room, and she could hear his feet hurrying down the stairs. She stood absolutely still until she heard the front door close. And then she sank back down onto the coverlet and closed her eyes. Actually, she did feel exhausted. And she wanted nothing more than to pull the covers over her head and forget all about Matt Lyons. But she wasn't going to permit herself to wallow in that sort of self-pity. Standing up again, she found her slippers and picked up the lovely blue-and-silver creation she'd worn so joyously for Matt—could it have been only the night before? It seemed like an eternity ago now. Smoothing its crumpled folds, she hung it back up in her closet and wondered if she'd ever wear it again. Right now she doubted it.

Turning away, she picked up the breakfast tray with its half-eaten toast and eggs and carried it back down to the kitchen. But her composure finally slipped away when she stepped across the threshold and spied the remains of last night's romantic dinner and Matt's breakfast preparations this morning. Her shoulders slumped as she took in the empty sparkling burgundy bottle on the counter, the fine china and silver stacked in an unwashed pile next to it, and the vase from which Matt had taken the rose for the breakfast tray. Looking down into its vibrant pink heart, she inhaled its lingering sweetness. She knew why Matt had chosen that particular flower. It had been a bud last night and was now the freshest of the blooms she'd brought in from the garden. Setting down the tray on the table, she opened the trash can and dumped the others in. But her hand hesitated over the deep pink rose in the crystal bud vase. She couldn't bring herself to throw that out. Instead, she carried it to the library. Glancing through its full shelves, she selected a novel that had been one of her favorites as a young girl. Opening it to the center, she laid the rose carefully inside, closed the volume again, and replaced it where she'd found it.

It was lucky that most of Sarah's preparations for the New York show had been completed before Matt's departure. In the three weeks that followed, she was able to get very little done. Just wedging clay seemed like too much

147

effort. She'd known she was going to miss him. But the pain of his absence was far worse than she'd anticipated. During their earlier breach, she'd been disturbed by his close proximity. Now it was his absence that made life seem gray. A hundred times her hand hovered over the phone. What if she called Matt to ask how the film was going? After all, it was a natural enough question. But he hadn't suggested she call him until she arrived in New York. That probably meant he didn't want to hear from her, Sarah told herself. And she was too proud to make the first move. The only hope she had now was that when she arrived in New York and they saw each other again, Matt would realize that he had missed her. It was a frail hope, but it was something to hang onto.

And yet, when she finally stood in her hotel room at the St. Regis unpacking the fashionably sophisticated ensembles she'd brought along, she knew that she'd been picturing herself wearing them for Matt rather than the audience at the East Side gallery where her works would soon be on view.

Sarah's thoughts were interrupted by the shrill ring of the phone.

"Hi there, gorgeous! Welcome to the Big Apple," Gordon Wentworth's smooth voice greeted her when she lifted the receiver.

"Perfect timing, I'm just about unpacked," Sarah returned, trying to match the enthusiasm in Gordon's voice.

"I thought you'd want to know that you did a fantastic job of packing your pieces. Everything arrived unscathed and that sculpture you call *Dream Woman* really knocked me out. It's just exactly what you needed for the focal point of the exhibit. It shows how much you've come of age as an artist."

Sarah found herself smiling at the receiver as she absorbed Gordon's words of praise. *Dream Woman* was something she still felt really good about. It was a solid achievement that she would be proud of all her life.

"I can't wait to show you how everything's been set up. How about dinner tonight and then afterward we'll do the gallery."

There was no use trying to make other plans when Gordon had his mind set on something. "Where shall I meet you?" Sarah inquired.

Three hours later she was sitting in a velvet-tufted banquette across the table from him at one of New York's understatedly elegant restaurants.

"Hard work must be good for you, Sarah. You've lost a bit of weight, but you look absolutely great—even more beautiful than I remember you."

Sarah smiled as she acknowledged the compliment. Gordon didn't know that it had taken a skilled makeup job to cover the circles under her eyes and bring color to her cheeks. And it was a pity men didn't wear makeup. Gordon was looking pale, tense, and slightly overweight. He would have been the better for a bit of flesh-toned cover-up to hide the shadows under his eyes.

"I've missed you, babe," he told her after they'd ordered drinks. "In fact, if I hadn't been so caught up in this rat race, I would have come up to the Cape to give you some encouragement—not that you needed it, of course."

Despite herself, Sarah had to suppress a grin. She could just imagine Gordon's reaction if he'd walked in on her and Matt at some strategic moment. But his discomfiture would not have mattered that much to her, she realized. Although she'd once thought of Gordon as more than a friend, that was definitely no longer the case. Before this trip was over, she'd have to let Gordon know that clearly. It wasn't fair not to understand where you stood with someone, she added wryly to herself. But there was no reason to spoil this dinner together with that sort of explanation. It could wait until later.

149

However, Gordon did not give her that luxury. "You know I've been thinking about you constantly, Sarah," he began after the waiter had brought their after-dinner coffee. "You've grown so much as an artist that handling you could turn into a full-time job. I've a feeling your work will really be in demand after this show."

Sarah added cream to her china cup and stirred it carefully. What was he getting at? she wondered as she watched the rich liquid swirl into the hot drink.

"You know, if you and I were married, it would make a lot of things easier for both of us. I wouldn't have to miss you when you get caught up in the creative process and shut the world out. And you'd have me around all the time to advise you and take care of things. I think it might be a really successful arrangement, Sarah. What do you think?"

Too stunned to speak, Sarah carefully put the spoon down on her saucer. Had she heard him right? Had Gordon just proposed marriage? And was he outlining the proposition as some sort of business arrangement? She did owe him a lot. He'd seen the promise in her work and guided her career. At one time she'd even thought they might mean something more to each other. But now that idea seemed ludicrous. It wasn't only her feelings for Matt. It was the crass way Gordon had just painted the picture of what he'd expected out of their marriage.

Firmly, Sarah began to shake her head. "Gordon, I don't know what to say. You know how much your friendship has meant to me. You were there when I needed somebody. But marriage between us just wouldn't work."

Gordon looked momentarily surprised. "Why not?"

Sarah could see from the tense expression on his face that this wasn't going to be easy. Taking a deep breath, she forced herself to plunge ahead. "After Brad and I broke up, I told myself I'd never marry again. And I don't have any reason to change my mind." Six weeks ago that might

150

have been a lie, she acknowledged inwardly. She had dared to entertain the fantasy of marriage with Matt. But since that final parting, she'd recognized that longing for the fantasy it was.

Gordon was scrutinizing her with narrowed eyes and, looking across at him, she suddenly realized what a savvy and tenacious opponent he must be at a negotiating table. Like a bulldog who'd sunk his teeth in, he wasn't going to let this go. "What's happened to you, Sarah? You've changed over the summer. You used to call me with progress reports, sometimes twice or three times during the week." As he spoke, Gordon leaned forward in his chair, folded his hands in an arch, and stared at her sharply. "But you stopped phoning, and I had to call you. And you sounded different on the phone, too—as though your mind were somewhere else."

In reaction, Sarah's gaze skidded away from his, and she pushed herself back in her chair. She didn't want to meet his penetrating look because it was seeing too much. And then she sighed. She had been trying to turn his proposal away kindly. But her attempt at diplomacy was backfiring, and the best course now was honesty.

"Gordon," she began, "you know me too well. You're right, something did happen this summer that changed things for me. I met a man—"

"I knew it!" Gordon interrupted. "That had to be it. Who is he?"

Sarah felt herself flushing. "You might know of him, as a matter of fact. He's a filmmaker who's doing a documentary on my father. His name is Matt Lyons!"

Gordon's features began to darken, and his pale blue eyes turned icy. "Matt Lyons," he muttered. "Of course I know who he is. Everyone in the business has heard of the golden boy of videotape. And I do mean *boy*," he emphasized with a sneer. "He must be several years younger than you, Sarah. What are you thinking of?"

Sarah stiffened. She couldn't deny that question had troubled her, too, even though Matt had convinced her it was a needless objection. But he'd left her after all. Could the four-year difference between them have had anything to do with his decision? Well, she certainly wasn't going to voice those doubts to the tight-lipped businessman eyeing her so critically now. "I'm not going to discuss it with you."

"Why not?" Gordon demanded. And then he raised a bushy eyebrow. "Matt Lyons isn't just known for his cinematographic talents. I've heard he's been a favorite in a lot of ladies' beds. Has he left you already?"

Sarah began to gather up her purse. "Thank you for a lovely dinner, Gordon. I'll see you at the gallery opening tomorrow," she clipped out coolly before getting up and hurrying toward the exit.

CHAPTER TEN

The beginning of the summer had held so much promise, Sarah thought unhappily as she tried once again to find a comfortable position in her unfamiliar hotel bed. It was hard to remember the exhilaration she'd felt when she'd started preparing for the show that was going to bring her name to the attention of the New York critics. Now that it was at hand, her excitement had almost completely evaporated.

Too much had happened too quickly. There had been the shattering discovery of those letters from Marjorie Winter, which had turned Sarah's happy memories of her family life into a cruel mockery. And then there was Matt. It was frightening how quickly he had become the focal point on the canvas of her life, like a brilliant dash of color. When he had taken that brightness away, she felt as though she were left with nothing but the dull background. And now that she was trying to adjust to life without him, there was this disturbing development with Gordon. He'd been not only her agent but a buttress of stability in her life. Why couldn't he have just left things the way they'd always been? she asked herself, rolling over and clutching the pillow to her chest. What was she going to do now? After this, they probably couldn't work together anymore, and she'd have to find a new agent.

But who was she kidding? she asked herself. It was really the unresolved relationship with Matt that was driving her crazy. Did he intend to see her again? Or was their parting on Cape Cod meant to be final? She had been too afraid of being rejected to ask him at the time. But the weeks of separation had made her realize that her own fears and self-doubts might have a lot to do with the breach in the relationship. From Matt's point of view, it might have seemed as if she had actually sent him away that morning. And if she had done that, maybe it was she who would have to make the first move now. Or maybe she'd simply been reading her own doubts into Matt's long silence. Maybe he really was swamped with work and would be glad if she made the first move. After all, hadn't he invited her to come see the film about her father when she was in New York? Suddenly Sarah knew she would have to do just that. She simply couldn't live with the uncertainty of things the way they were.

Once she had made the decision, she was eager to follow it up. But it was too late tonight for anything of the kind. And tomorrow must be spent at the gallery until almost dinnertime. She would drop in on Matt, though, as soon as she could get away.

Sarah yawned. Now that she'd decided on a course of action, she was suddenly sleepy. And a good thing, too. The day that would follow at the Vasholz Gallery would be an exhausting one.

For the first time in weeks, Sarah was able to enjoy breakfast. Dressed for autumn in New York in a soft navy suit with a vivid print blouse pinned in an ascot at the neck, she stopped off at a little patisserie around the corner from her hotel. Over buttery croissants and coffee, she read the announcement of her show in the Arts and Leisure section of *The New York Times*. Seeing her name in print was a heady feeling. And suddenly she wondered if Matt might have seen it, too. Buoyed up by the idea, she took a taxi to the elegantly appointed Vasholz. There were not many young artists who could lay claim to a first New

York show in such prestigious surroundings, she thought as she pushed open one of the heavy, black glass and polished chrome doors.

With its thick gray carpeting and off-white textured walls, the Vasholz provided the perfect setting for Sarah's work. Her colorful glazed sculptures and cast bronze pieces had been artfully arranged on smoked lucite pedestals of different heights. Lighted individually, each seemed to hold a place of honor. And yet *Dream Woman* was the centerpiece, somehow bringing everything else together. On its broad, white marble base, it dominated the room and drew the eye. And Sarah couldn't hold back the smile of satisfaction that lifted her mouth as she took in the end result of months of work and aspiration.

"I recognize you from your picture. You must be that talented young woman, Sarah Kiteredge," a heavily accented voice to her right ventured. I'm Walter Vasholz and I'm honored to welcome you to my gallery."

Sarah turned and smiled warmly at the tall, aristocratic-looking gentleman in the immaculately tailored dark suit who had greeted her. "I'm the one who's honored," she told him with complete sincerity. I can't even begin to tell you what a thrill all this is for me." As she spoke, she gestured around at the tastefully arranged display.

"Ah, but it was so easy to set up this display. Such wonderful pieces. They've only been here a week, and already I've sold several—including that fantastic *Dream Woman.*"

Sarah stared at him in astonishment. Not really wanting to sell *Dream Woman,* she had set such an outrageous price on it that she'd assumed no one would be interested. "Can you tell me who bought it?" she questioned now. "Unfortunately, no. My assistant who handled the transaction is off on a buying trip. She must have been so astonished to make such a major sale even before the exhibit officially opened that she forgot to write down the buyer's name. But she'll be back next week, and you'll be able to ask her about it then."

Sarah sighed. She didn't know whether to be glad or disappointed. But she hated to spoil Walter Vasholz's obvious pleasure.

"I expect this to be a busy day. The caterer is already in back setting up. There will be a plenty of champagne, which ought to loosen up the critics, not that they'll need it. One look at your work and I'm sure they'll be as excited as I am."

Sarah smiled her thanks and then strolled with him into the main exhibit area. Off to one side, the caterers were busy arranging festive little hors d'oeuvres and a tray of fresh fruit on a starched linen tablecloth. "The shrimp and caviar must still be in the back," Mr. Vasholz remarked.

"This is so much more than I expected. I'm overwhelmed," Sarah told him.

"It's nothing. Your initial sales have already more than paid for this spread. So I suggest you just relax and enjoy your triumph before things get too hectic."

The advice was excellent. It was a good thing that Sarah sampled some of the goodies the caterers had arranged before lunchtime, because, by twelve thirty, the gallery was swamped with critics and patrons eager for her attention. She was so busy that she didn't even have time to worry about Gordon, who came in during the rush and was holding court in another corner of the room. The crush didn't abate until almost three o'clock. And by that time Sarah felt a strange mixture of exhaustion and exhilaration. Never in her wildest dreams had she expected her work to command so much attention. And she was feeling a little giddy.

Not knowing how long the lull would last, she poured herself a cup of coffee and leaned against one of the richly textured walls. She had just taken a grateful sip of the hot beverage when a flurry of motion at the other side of the

156

room made her glance up. When she saw who had entered the gallery and was walking purposefully toward her, Sarah swallowed the hot beverage too quickly and it burned as it went down her throat. It was Marjorie Winter. The still spectacular blonde was dressed in a dramatic-looking peacock blue suit and matching hat. And as she moved across the lushly carpeted floor with fluid grace, Sarah almost dropped her cup and then turned to set it carefully on the table next to her. What in the world was her father's former mistress doing at her show? Sarah wondered, her eyes darting around the room as though looking for an escape route.

But it was obvious that there was no escape. Marjorie was heading straight for her, a brilliant smile curving the lines of her carefully painted mouth. She was certainly well preserved, Sarah noted. She had to give her that. The woman must be close to fifty, and she could have passed for thirty-five. In her day she had been one of Hollywood's most beautiful starlets. Unlike some, she had maintained her face and figure carefully. Eyeing her, Sarah could almost understand what had captivated her father. There was an aura of sensuality and vivacious energy that Sarah sensed even before the woman spoke to her. Unlike Sarah's mother who had never really let herself enjoy life, Marjorie was obviously a woman who drained every last drop.

"My dear," she exclaimed, coming forward and seizing Sarah's limp hand, "when I saw the notice of your show in *The Times,* I just couldn't stay away. To think of Wallace's little girl winning this kind of recognition. He would have been so proud of you, dear. It brings tears to my eyes to think that he didn't live to be here for this." And sure enough, Sarah could see that there really were tears glistening in Marjorie's Wedgwood-blue eyes.

Despite herself, Sarah felt some of her enmity leaking away. When she'd read those letters she'd hated Marjorie

Winter. But now that she was actually in the woman's presence, it wasn't so easy. Obviously, the actress was still grieving over Wallace Kiteredge's death. And how could Sarah really hate a person who had sincerely loved someone she had loved—even if that lost loved one was her own father?

Sarah nodded. "I guess I like to think that, wherever he is, Dad knows about this. . . . I wanted so much for him to be proud of me."

Marjorie squeezed her hand sympathetically. "He was proud of you, dear, even if he wasn't always around to let you know it. He used to talk to me about you."

Sarah blanched, and Marjorie was perceptive enough to notice. "You know that your father and I were good friends for many years, don't you?"

Sarah's jaw felt tight. "Yes," she managed.

A frown began to wrinkle the actress's smooth brow. "Oh, my dear," she exclaimed softly, taking a step backward and giving Sarah an appraising look. "I think you've gotten the wrong idea about Wallace and me." She watched Sarah's expression closely, then said, "You and I need to talk. But this isn't the place." She glanced around at the small crowd that still filled the gallery. "I'm going to be in the city for the next few days. Tell me where you're staying, Sarah, and we'll plan to have dinner."

Sarah wasn't sure how to react. Part of her wanted no more contact with Marjorie Winter. But another side of her argued that it was only fair to hear her out. The truth was that she really did want to know more about her father's relationship with the actress. After finding those letters, her imagination had run wild. No matter how painful, it would be better to know the truth.

"All right," she agreed. "I'm staying at the St. Regis. Would tomorrow night be a good time for you?"

"Perfect," Marjorie concurred. "I'll call you tomorrow to confirm our plans."

If the encounter with Marjorie had been unsettling, there was even more reason for Sarah to feel nervous as the long day in the gallery drew to a close. Last night when she'd made the decision to go see Matt, she'd felt relieved. But now her stomach was knotting in nervous anticipation. Maybe she should have called first, she told herself. But there simply hadn't been time. And she didn't want to talk to him over the phone, anyway. She wanted to be able to see his face so that she could read his expression. That would give her a much better chance of knowing what his true feelings really were.

"You look awfully tired," Walter Vasholz told her, tapping her slender shoulder gently. "Why don't you call it a day?"

Sarah thanked him gratefully. Being on her feet and smiling constantly now seemed like harder work than producing the sculptures that everyone had come to see.

Stopping in the small restroom to comb her hair and renew her makeup, Sarah eyed her reflection critically. She did look tired. She'd lost weight in the last month, and her cheeks were pale from the strain of the long day. But beyond dabbing on a bit of blusher, there wasn't much to be done about that now. If she went back to her hotel room to rest, she might get cold feet and put the whole thing off. After checking the address of his apartment and studio in the phone book, she said her good-byes to Mr. Vasholz and headed up to the avenue to look for a cab.

But it was hard to get one this late in the afternoon, and New York's rush-hour traffic was so turgid that she didn't arrive at the address she'd jotted down until well past five.

It turned out to be a large warehouse, and Sarah wondered if she'd made a mistake. But when she stepped inside, she realized the building had been converted into an attractive complex of offices and studios. However, many of the original architectural elements had been retained. The big old elevator she took up to Matt's top-floor enclave had previously been used for freight. And when she stepped out and looked up, she could see a bank of wire-reinforced skylights that must have been part of the original building. On the other hand, all of the rough-sawed paneling above the wide, old-fashioned baseboards had to be new. Together, the melding of architectural elements from different periods made an attractive whole. Though Sarah admired the tasteful decor, she was too apprehensive about the coming encounter between her and Matt to give much thought to anything else.

When she finally stood before the door bearing his name on a brass plate, she took several deep breaths before knocking. When there was no answer, she finally pushed it open and walked into a small reception area furnished with a wide teak desk and several comfortable-looking leather lounge chairs. She stood for a moment looking at the colorful framed posters that decorated the walls and wondered if anyone was about. Just then, however, a door behind the desk opened, and a friendly-looking young man with a thatch of dark brown hair came out.

He stopped in the act of setting a folder down on the desk and looked at Sarah in surprise. "I was just about to leave, but can I help you?"

Sarah shifted the weight of her shoulder bag. "I'm Sarah Kiteredge. I came to see Matt Lyons. Is he in?"

The young man's boyish face lit up. "Oh, yes. I should have recognized you from the footage I've just been going over. But you look different when you don't have your hair in pigtails," he added with a grin, and Sarah knew he was referring to some tape Matt had shot of her on the beach just before he left. "Hi, I'm Jerry Stovall," he volunteered, holding out his hand.

Smiling, Sarah shook it. "How's the film coming?" she asked, sounding much more casual than she felt. While she'd been making the final preparations for the show, she'd put the film out of her mind. But now all the concerns she'd had about it resurfaced.

"It's almost done. In fact," he added, glancing at his wristwatch, "if you have the time, Matt should be back in about an hour. You know he lives here, too, so he's usually around."

Sarah nodded.

"I have to go now," the young man continued. "But I could set the videotape up for you and you could watch it while you wait."

Sarah agreed instantly. "That would be perfect."

Jerry put his hand on the doorknob and then turned back toward Sarah, his thin face clouding slightly. "Maybe I spoke a bit too hastily," he began. "Matt really doesn't like to have his work in progress shown, but since you've been involved in the project, I guess it'll be okay."

As she followed him through the door into a large workroom, Sarah nibbled on her lower lip. For a moment she wondered if she was invading Matt's privacy. After all, she hadn't wanted him to see *Dream Woman*. But this was different. The subject of his film was her father, and she had cooperated in providing a lot of the background information. *I have every right to see it,* she told herself as she sat down in front of the monitor the young man indicated.

She waited nervously while he rewound the tape and, in a few minutes, the credits were beginning to flash onto the screen over the background picture of a sloop being buffeted about in the wind. It was as effective an opening as Matt had predicted, she thought, leaning back in her chair. She was so absorbed in the images flashing across the screen that she didn't even notice when Jerry closed the door quietly behind him as he left.

The first scenes were of her father's early life, and Sarah found herself marveling at the skillful way Matt interwove the black-and-white photographs she'd given him with color footage of the same scenes. Following these were

161

brief clips from early movies her father had made with his boyhood friends and then still photographs he'd taken for an advertising firm in New York. Much of this material was new to Sarah and she was fascinated. She'd assumed that she'd supplied the bulk of Matt's background. But apparently he had been much more resourceful than she'd realized. *If he'd wanted to, he could have made this film without me,* she thought. *Getting in touch with me was more of a courtesy than a necessity. He must have done almost all of his research before even coming to the Cape.* The thought was reassuring. It meant that her relationship with Matt had not really been based on exploitation. Sarah relaxed into her chair even more, ready to enjoy the rest of the film as much as she had the beginning.

The next shots were footage of her family's early life together. She saw home movies of herself and her mother in the backyard of their house in Santa Monica. These were followed by old footage of Hollywood just after the war and of the old Global back lots in Studio City. And then there were scenes from her father's first feature film.

"There was nothing remarkable about the screenplay for *Son of the Alamo*," the narrator explained. "It took Wallace Kiteredge's unique insight and creativity to carry the story beyond the realm of the run-of-the-mill Western."

It was then that a cheesecake shot of Marjorie Winter as a gorgeous young starlet flashed on the screen. Sarah's eyes opened wide and she sat up straight in her leather chair.

"But it wasn't until after he met lovely young Marjorie Winter that his artistic vision really blossomed. A long and enduring friendship developed between the young starlet and the fledgling director . . ."

Sarah's mind had stopped taking in the narrative. And all she could do was stare in frozen horror at the series of black-and-white pictures of her father and the actress as

162

they worked together on the set of some film or other. But when a color image of the actress as she looked now suddenly appeared on the screen, the ice that seemed to encase Sarah's body cracked. Jumping up, she stormed toward the monitor and snapped it off, leaving the tape running in the machine. She could feel her heart pounding in her throat. Why had Matt done this to her? What did he hope to accomplish? But she already knew the answer to that. He wanted to make a film that would get noticed. And by sensationalizing her father's private life, he would probably accomplish his purpose. It was one thing to rake up the personal peccadilloes of someone like Walt Whitman who had been dead for almost a century. It was quite another to make a gossip's free-for-all out of her father's past. Maybe Matt didn't care about how this would affect Marjorie Winter. But hadn't he thought about what this kind of publicity would do to her and Bev?

But then Sarah's mouth tightened into a grim line. Matt wasn't stupid. No, indeed, he was a very smart cookie. He must have thought about the consequences of this film and simply decided that he didn't care—so long as it accomplished what he wanted for himself and his career.

For a moment, her eyes went to the still-whirring video recorder. What if she took the tape out and simply disappeared with it? But then she shook her head. What good would that do? It couldn't be the only copy. Still, what if she took it to a lawyer? Was there some way she could sue Matt to keep him from showing it?

Kneeling down in front of the formidable-looking machine, she studied the buttons and switches that controlled it. She'd never operated anything quite like this. If she started fooling with it, she might break something. But then the knot in her stomach tightened, and she clenched her teeth. Matt had certainly not taken any pains not to hurt her. What did she care if she broke his damn machine?

163

She had just pushed the button marked STOP/EJECT and retrieved the cassette when the door in back of her opened.

Holding the plastic cassette in her hand, Sarah whirled around, knowing the expression on her face was guilty. But as Matt Lyons strode into the room, he was too busy taking in her presence to register her emotions. Though she hadn't known he was coming back so soon, she had been prepared for his eventual return. He, on the other hand, hadn't expected her to be here. Sarah's automatic guilt reaction changed to anger. But Matt saw none of this. When he recognized the woman in his studio, he stopped in his tracks, and his face broke into a wide smile.

"Sarah, when did you get here? God, it's so great to see you!" As he spoke, he moved toward her, holding out his arms.

But his welcoming smile withered when he began to register the expression on Sarah's face. She had risen and was facing him like a duelist on the field of honor.

Matt halted his progress across the room and stared at her questioningly. "What is it? What's wrong?" And then his gaze dropped to the tape in her hand. "Did Jerry set the videotape up for you?"

"Jerry was very accommodating," Sarah clipped out in a frigid voice.

Matt studied her, the emerald green of his eyes clouded with puzzlement. "I knew it was rough," he began, "but you look like it's the worst thing since *The Attack of the Killer Tomatoes.*"

Sarah was far from amused. "I'd rather have seen just about anything than what you've got on that tape of yours," she clipped out in a frozen voice, her knuckles whitening on the clear black plastic cassette. "How could you do this, Matt? I trusted you, and all the time you were just making a fool of me!"

"What do you mean—" Matt began.

164

But Sarah cut him off. "Oh, come on. Don't pretend that you don't know what I'm talking about. How could you drag Marjorie Winter into this? How could you expose my whole family to ridicule?"

Matt's own countenance had begun to harden. "Did you look at the whole thing, or are you jumping to conclusions?" he demanded.

"I saw quite enough," Sarah shot back, grabbing her purse and stuffing the cassette into it. "I'm going to show this to a lawyer."

Matt's eyebrows shot up. "Lawyer? I'm afraid you'd better tell me exactly what you mean."

Like a cornered animal getting ready to defend itself, Sarah had gone white. She didn't even notice that her hands and feet were icy. "I don't have to explain myself to you, but I will, anyway. You did nothing but use and exploit me on the Cape. All you wanted was to sensationalize my father's life and drag my family name through the mud to advance your own career. Well, you're not going to get away with it if I can help it. If there's some legal way of stopping you from using this film, I'll find it."

At the accusation, Matt's own anger flared up to match hers. And his eyes began to flash green fire. "So that's it," he ground out. "You haven't even seen the whole tape and you're jumping to conclusions. After everything, you have no faith in me at all."

Sarah's mouth tightened. "You're awfully good at talking your way out of situations, but you're not going to do it this time, Matt."

"Don't worry," he shot back. "I could talk till I'm blue in the face and nothing I say would mean a thing to you. You've never trusted me or believed me. You're a fine one to talk about ethics. You only slept with me because you wanted to control my work!"

Sarah's jaw dropped open. "Why, you insulting . . ." she began.

165

But Matt was not about to stay and listen. Turning on his heels, he strode from the room, leaving her standing with her purse clutched in her hand.

For a moment she stood there in the empty studio, wondering what to do next. But when she finally poked her head into the anteroom, no one was in sight. Feeling like a trespasser, she scurried across the carpeted floor of the outer office and then into the hall. That was empty, too.

Shakily, Sarah made her way out of the deserted building. All the adrenaline that had given her the strength to stand up to Matt had leaked away, leaving her weak and disoriented. Her legs were so rubbery that she wondered if she'd be able to make it to the end of the block. Luckily, at that moment, a taxi passed and she was able to hail it.

"You look like you've been hit by a steamroller, lady," the cheeky cab driver commented as she crawled into the backseat. "Where to?"

"The St. Regis," Sarah muttered faintly before leaning back in the seat and shutting her eyes. Had that horrible scene in Matt's office really happened? she asked herself. But it had. There was no denying the video cassette shoved into her purse. She could feel its outline against the soft leather, and the shape was still burning itself into her palm when she had finally gained the sanctuary of her room.

CHAPTER ELEVEN

The confrontation with Matt had been so shattering that Sarah begged off spending the day at the gallery. In fact, just getting out of bed and ordering room service for lunch seemed like a major effort—and a wasted one, at that. The chicken salad sandwich she ordered tasted like cardboard, and it was all she could do to force down a few bites and sip her coffee while she scanned a newspaper. In the arts section there was a glowing review of her work. But all the pleasure she had thought such a favorable critique would elicit never materialized. It didn't seem to matter anymore. In fact, nothing seemed to matter.

After lunch she left the hotel and walked along Fifth Avenue, staring into glossy shop windows without really seeing anything but her pale reflection. She hadn't bothered to put on any makeup. And it probably wouldn't help now, anyway. When she returned to her room, the signal light on her phone was flashing. Who would be calling her? she wondered. It certainly wasn't Matt. That little affair was all over.

The message turned out to be from Gordon, congratulating her on the favorable review. But she didn't feel like replying. Instead, she sat down tiredly by the window and looked down at the crawling traffic and hurrying pedestrians. New York seemed like such an alien place. What was she doing here, anyway? Her presence at the gallery was no longer required. She might as well pack up and go home.

But even making arrangements to leave seemed like too much effort. And, besides, she'd have to talk to Walter Vasholz and Gordon before going. That, too, might as well have been an impossible undertaking.

The day slid by in a gray haze. And it wasn't until a call came in from Marjorie Winter that Sarah remembered their dinner engagement.

"I know I suggested a restaurant, but that's ridiculous. Why don't you come to my place at the Dakota."

Sarah's first impulse was to beg off. After seeing that film, Marjorie was the last person—no, the second to last person—she wanted to have dinner with tonight. Though Sarah couldn't understand Marjorie's reasons for doing so, she knew the actress must have cooperated with Matt.

But when Sarah began to politely refuse, the older woman made it impossible. "I think I have the right to give you my side of the story, Sarah. It's important to both of us. I'll send a car around for you at six thirty."

Despite her reluctance to see anyone—particularly Marjorie Winter—there was no way Sarah could refuse that kind of request. Though it was hard to make herself go through the motions of getting ready, Sarah forced herself to pick out a flattering aqua dinner dress and a pair of chic, black-patterned panty hose. After a long, soothing soak in the hotel's oversize tub, she coaxed her hair into a becoming upsweep and began to make up her face. Marjorie Winter was an attractive woman who was very carefully packaged. And as long as Sarah had to confront her, she didn't want to be at a disadvantage on that score.

Nevertheless, when she crossed the actress's marble threshold, it was impossible not to find the surroundings intimidating. Entering the famous, fortresslike building that overlooked Central Park was like surrendering to the enemy. Once Sarah was past its high iron gate, she looked around at its elaborate Victorian details. But the building itself was nothing compared to the interior of Marjorie's apartment. She had used the Victorian architectural details as a foil for her collection of French rococo furniture. Her large rooms were carpeted with Aubusson rugs and furnished entirely with antiques that would not have embarrassed even Louis XIV. The precious woods, carved in flowing shapes and ornamented with gilt, made Sarah wonder if the woman had raided Versailles. But Marjorie herself managed to be the focal point of the setting. Dressed in a flowing peach damask caftan with her golden hair loose around her proud shoulders, she could have been a queen granting an audience—or a king's mistress, Sarah couldn't help thinking with a touch of bitterness.

"My dear, I'm so glad you could come," Marjorie greeted her, gliding forward amid the swish of rich fabric.

To Sarah's relief, the actress led the way through a series of grand rooms into a small, private sitting room. Although furnished with equal expense, it was much cozier and far less intimidating. Sinking onto a white watered-silk love seat, Sarah gratefully accepted the glass of Chablis that Marjorie proffered in a stunning crystal wineglass.

"You know, all this is just for show," Marjorie said with a sweep of her graceful hand. "You don't know how much advantage there is to greeting the press in a setting like this. The home I really prefer, of course, is my beach house in Carpinteria. Wallace used to love that place, too. He used to love to come there to unwind."

At the mention of her father, Sarah's hand tightened around the fragile stem of her wineglass.

Marjorie noticed the telltale gesture immediately. "Sarah, we both know that Hollywood gossip can be both poisonous and entirely false. I want to ask you a question. After your father died, did anyone say something about my relationship with him that made you think"—she paused, searching for a delicate way to continue—"that he had been, uh, disloyal to your mother?"

"What do you think?" Sarah retorted, unable to keep the bitter edge out of her voice.

The actress's steady aquamarine gaze never wavered. "I have to assume from your obvious hostility that they did."

"Well, you're wrong," Sarah shot back, setting her glass down on the small inlaid table between them. "No one had to tell me anything. He saved all those letters you sent him. And when I was going through his things in his Hollywood condominium, I found them."

For the first time during their conversation, the actress's composure seemed to slip. "Sarah, those letters don't mean what you think they do," she insisted, leaning forward and setting down her own glass. "Over the years, Wallace and I had a very special relationship. But it isn't what you're thinking."

But Sarah was on the attack now, and she couldn't hold back the hateful words that had been brewing in her head for so long now. "You mean you didn't carry on a twenty-year affair with him behind my mother's back? You mean your son Philip isn't really my half brother? You mean my father's real loyalty wasn't to *you* rather than to his family?"

In an uncharacteristic lapse, Marjorie's jaw dropped, and the blood seemed to drain from her face, making her suddenly look ten years older. "My God, is that what you've been thinking all these months?" she finally managed.

"How could I think anything else?" Sarah shot back. "And after I saw you in that tasteless film of Matt Lyons's, it was even more obvious. But how could you do it? You weren't just slinging mud at my father's reputation, you were blackening your own as well. And that doesn't make sense." Sarah sat tensely waiting for the actress to reply.

But Marjorie seemed to have been struck dumb. Getting up, she went to the window and stared out for a moment. Finally, she turned back to Sarah, a puzzled expression on her face. "I'm not sure what you mean about the Lyons film," she began hesitantly. "Are you sure you watched the whole thing?"

"I didn't have to watch the whole film," Sarah started to argue. But somehow she was feeling a bit more unsure of her position than she had five minutes ago.

"It's a pity we don't have a copy of the tape here," Marjorie went on. "There's no way I could explain my relationship with your father any better than I did for Matt. That man has a way of drawing out the best in anyone he interviews."

Convulsively, Sarah's hand went to her purse. The tape was still jammed into it. Though she'd threatened to take it to a lawyer, she hadn't even thought about it since leaving Matt's studio the evening before. Just what would the tape show? she wondered. Had her own stupid prejudice made her jump to some unwarranted conclusion? It hardly seemed possible. And yet, Marjorie had just spoken with such conviction . . ."

The actress saw the doubt flicker across her face and narrowed her eyes speculatively. "What is it, Sarah?" she asked.

Sarah hesitated for a moment, afraid of what the film might really show, and yet afraid not to find out now. "It happens that I have a copy in my purse," she finally owned up.

"A cassette?" Marjorie asked, crossing the room again and sitting down next to Sarah on the sofa.

"Yes," Sarah admitted, opening her handbag and fishing out the plastic cassette. "I took it out of the VCR in Matt's studio yesterday." She didn't add the part about the lawyer. Under the circumstances, it sounded just too acrimonious.

Marjorie's face lit up. "We can show it on my re-

171

corder," she said, pointing to an unobtrusive cabinet across the room.

Again Sarah hesitated, her fingers biting into the hard plastic. Did she want to go through with this? But she knew she did. It was mortifying to realize that she really had jumped to conclusions without watching the end of the film. "All right," she agreed in a small voice, handing over the evidence.

It took Marjorie only a moment to open the cabinet and load the cassette. "I take it you *have* seen the first part of the film?" she questioned, glancing at Sarah over her shoulder.

The younger woman could only nod.

"Then why don't I skip right to my interview," Marjorie suggested, beginning to run the tape on fast forward. When she got to the interview in question, she brought the picture down to normal speed.

Sarah didn't realize she was clutching the sofa arm as though holding on to a lifeline. Her whole body tensed as the actress began to speak. At first she was so nervous that she didn't hear the words. But after the first few sentences, they began to register.

"Wallace Kiteredge and I had a very special relationship," Marjorie was saying in the film, "because he was a very special person. When I first met him, I knew he wouldn't leave his wife and family. But I was madly in love with him, and if he'd asked me to become his mistress, I would probably have agreed."

Sarah's eyes widened, but they didn't leave the screen.

"But that's not what Wallace wanted," the actress continued. "His wife couldn't stand the Hollywood limelight and took the family back to Cape Cod. And because Wallace was alone so much of the time, he needed a friend and companion, someone he could talk to, someone with whom to share his artistic vision."

172

Sarah leaned forward, intent on catching every word now.

"I shared Wallace's hopes and dreams. Ours was a rare and wonderful friendship. And I'd like to think that I made a difference in his work."

There was more, but Sarah didn't need to hear. She turned around and stared questioningly at the actress. "Were you telling the truth?" she asked. "You and my father weren't lovers? Your son isn't my half brother?"

Marjorie nodded. "What I didn't say in public, of course, was the kind of temptation I must have presented to Wallace, alone and missing his wife and family."

Sarah swallowed and nodded.

"But he had too much integrity to betray his marriage vows. Though I loved him, we were never more than deep and close friends. My son Philip is no relation to you—although he could have been if Wallace had wished it. But Philip belongs to another part of my life, a part I created when I couldn't get everything I needed from your father."

The tension that had been holding Sarah rigid seemed to ebb away, and she sagged against the padded sofa back.

"I flatter myself that I did make a difference in your father's artistic life," Marjorie continued. "I was someone with whom he could discuss ideas—get reactions."

"Yes," Sarah agreed. She knew that her mother had never been that sort of companion. That was actually one of the reasons she had wanted to leave Hollywood. She just wasn't the kind of woman who could take a deep interest in artistic creation. But Marjorie hadn't said that —either on the tape or here in her private domain. She had come to terms with what Wallace had given, and she didn't need to discredit someone else to make her own position seem more important.

The actress appeared to read Sarah's thoughts. "There is one thing I do have some guilt about," she admitted. "I

173

didn't have a sexual relationship with your father, but there were times when I arranged things so that he would stay in Hollywood with me instead of going back to Cape Cod to his family. I think you do have reason to be upset with me on that count," she added, looking down at her carefully polished nails.

Sarah shook her head. "No, Marjorie. If he stayed in Hollywood with you, it was because he wanted to—not because you had some hold over him. I can see now that he got something from you, something he apparently wasn't able to get from anyone else."

The actress understood just how much that last utterance had cost Sarah. And now there were tears in the older woman's eyes. "I told myself that was true so many times. But it took Matt Lyons to make me really sure."

Sarah nodded, realizing what Matt's perception of her father's work had done for Marjorie. No matter what the actress had tried to tell herself about her relationship with Wallace Kiteredge, she had always felt some guilt. Matt had been able to show her how really important she was to the director.

It was yet another piece of information that was rapidly changing her perception of the man who had contrived to meet her on the beach just a few short months ago. And yet there were still questions in her mind.

"When did Matt find out about your friendship with my father?" she queried.

"I came to him when I heard he was making the documentary. I knew there were unpleasant rumors circulating about Wallace and me. And I wanted to set the record straight. Matt was eager to hear what I had to say. Wallace Kiteredge was one of his heroes, and he wanted his film to be a definitive portrait. When he started his research, there were things in Wallace's life that puzzled him. I was able to supply the missing pieces that allowed him to put together an accurate picture."

Sarah couldn't help looking down at her hands. And what role had she played in Matt's endeavor? she asked herself. Oh, sure, she'd taken him around and showed him her father's boyhood haunts. But her motives had been less than aboveboard. Matt was right, she had tried to stand in his way—to present a sanitized picture suitable for public consumption. But what a fool she'd been. That hadn't been necessary at all. In this case, truth was better than the false reality she'd tried so hard to create.

"I think I owe you an apology," Sarah mumbled, unable to meet Marjorie's bright blue eyes. "I've been thinking all sorts of evil things about you. And apparently none of them are true."

The actress shook her blond head. "No, part of this is my fault. I was so anxious to set the public record straight. But I should have thought that you might find out something about me and your father after his death. I should have come to you much earlier. If I had, none of this would have happened."

Sarah gave her a rueful smile. "I probably wouldn't have talked to you then," she admitted.

Marjorie took her hand. "You know, your father loved you very much. His relationship with his wife might not have been all that he had wished for, but you and your sister were very precious to him. He talked about you all the time. And he was so proud that you had so much artistic talent."

It was hard for Sarah to hold back the tears that threatened to spill down her cheeks. And Marjorie could see her deep emotion. Moving closer, she drew the younger woman into her arms. "You don't have to hold back with me. We both loved Wallace. We both lost a great deal when he died."

The floodgates Sarah had been struggling to hold closed finally collapsed under the pressure. For a long while she

175

could only weep quietly on Marjorie's shoulder. Finally, however, the emotional storm abated.

"Are you still too upset to have dinner?" Marjorie asked. "If you are, I can easily give you a rain check."

Sarah shook her head. "I'm not too upset. But there's someone else I have to apologize to."

Marjorie didn't ask whom the younger woman was referring to. But it was obvious that she suspected. "Well, then, good luck, my dear," she offered with an encouraging pat on Sarah's shoulder. "Do you want me to call you a cab?" she added.

Sarah nodded and then went to repair her makeup as best she could. When she had finished, she stood back to take a critical look at herself. Her eyes were still a bit red. But the overall effect of the emotional release was salutary. A great weight had been lifted from her shoulders, making it easier to face whatever lay ahead with Matt.

Fifteen minutes later she was on her way to his studio. But as her cab made its slow progress across town, she began to doubt the wisdom of this impulsive course of action. Matt might not even be home. And what if he were? What would he say? Or, more to the point, what would she say? And what did she want?

That last thought brought a lump to her throat. She knew what she wanted. She wanted Matt's forgiveness. She wanted his love. She wanted the things she now knew he had been offering all along—the things that she had been too blind to see before and too afraid to try to win. Now she knew that if you never dare, you never get your heart's desire.

The lump in her throat had grown larger, making it hard to breathe. Sarah leaned back against the vinyl seat and closed her eyes. It might already be too late for what she wanted with Matt. She had flung some pretty terrible words at him yesterday—words that it might be hard to forgive. But whatever his reaction, she knew that she had to go ahead with this apology, if only to asuage her own guilty conscience. Even if he wouldn't take her back, she owed him that. And if he weren't home tonight, then she'd simply try again tomorrow.

Yet, when they had pulled up in front of his studio, she hesitated. This was not the best neighborhood for a woman alone at night. And there wasn't a lot of traffic. If she sent the cab away, would she be able to get another one?

"Would you mind waiting for me?" she asked the driver. "I may be right back."

"It's your dime, lady," he informed her, apparently not even interested enough to inquire about the reason for her request.

Although the man himself was small comfort, Sarah was glad he was waiting as she pushed open the door of Matt's building and headed for the elevator. It was all she could do to keep herself from turning around and asking to be driven to her hotel. But she wasn't going to do that, she told herself as she waited nervously for the slow-moving car to reach the first floor. She was going to see this thing through, no matter what the cost.

However, when she finally stood in front of Matt's door, she had to take several deep breaths before she could force herself to raise her hand and knock. Her first effort was so timid that it was barely audible. So she summoned up her courage and tried again—this time so forcefully that her knuckles smarted. Still, there was no answer. Had she come all this way for nothing, after all? Sarah asked herself, turning to leave. But she just couldn't give up quite yet. Balling her hand into a fist, she gave the door several hard clouts and was just putting her weight into another when the door suddenly swung open. Thrown off balance, Sarah tumbled forward and was stopped from falling only by the barrier of Matt Lyons's chest, which happened to be covered by a crisply starched dress shirt.

"What?" he began in surprise, as an embarrassed Sarah tried to regain her footing and her composure.

When he realized who had just crashed into him, the tone of his voice changed. "What are you trying to do, break down my damn door?" he demanded, his brows snapping together in an angry line. The look he gave her would have frozen boiling water.

In the cab on the way over, Sarah had tried to prepare herself for an angry reception. But the reality of facing a scowling, belligerent Matt was much worse than she had imagined. It took all her courage to keep from turning and slinking out of sight. But she wasn't going to let him sway her from her purpose so easily.

"May I come in and talk to you for a minute?" she asked with as much dignity as she could muster.

"Anything you have to say to me can be said right here in the hall," he shot back, shifting his position so that his body blocked the doorway.

Sarah was unable to meet his eyes. Instead she focused somewhere in the vicinity of his belt buckle. He was wearing charcoal wool slacks with front pleats, she noted irrelevantly. He smelled of soap and lemon aftershave lotion. Sarah realized she must have caught him on his way out. Apparently he had shrugged off the effects of yesterday's scene. And if she hadn't appeared at his door to refocus his anger, he wouldn't have spared any thought for her this evening. The realization made her chest tighten painfully. For she knew now that any tender feelings he had once had for her were now dead.

That certain knowledge should have made her task easier. After all, what did all this matter anymore? Yet she found it almost impossible to bring her own emotions under control.

"Matt," she began again, barely able to manage more than a whisper.

"Speak up, dammit. I can't hear you." Now that she

had intruded upon him, he seemed bent upon making this interview as hard as possible for her.

Sarah laced her fingers together to keep her hands from trembling. The only way she was going to be able to get out what she wanted to say was to do it quickly and then just leave.

"Well?" Matt prompted, the syllable an angry rumble in his chest.

"I–I wanted to tell you I was wrong," she stammered. "I went back and looked at the part of the film, the part where, the part . . ." She had to stop for a moment and pull together all the self-discipline she had left. "I–I wanted to apologize because . . ." she tried again. But that was all she could get out without breaking down and making a complete fool of herself.

Quickly she turned, afraid he would see the pain written across her face. Her vision was blurred by tears now. But she could make out the red exit sign at the end of the hall. She would take the stairs. She couldn't imagine waiting for the elevator with Matt's bitter gaze boring into the back of her head.

Shoulders sagging and head bowed, she turned and started away. The sound of her own heels clicking on the tile floor seemed to reverberate through the whole hallway. Why didn't Matt close the door and go back inside? part of her mind wondered. Why was he standing there looking at her? Was he enjoying this somehow?

And then to her confusion, she could hear another sound, as though bare feet were pounding down the hall after her. In the next second, a rock-hard hand had grasped her shoulder and spun her around so that there was no way to hide her tear-streaked face from Matt's piercing green gaze.

"*Why* did you want to apologize?" he demanded.

She could only stare at him blankly.

"*Why?*" he persisted.

"I—I owed it to you." The last word was a sort of gulp before her voice cracked completely. Shaking her head, she looked away, knowing she had no control left. She could feel tears running freely down her face now. Was he just going to stand here with his hand on her shoulder, making her suffer? If she could have asked him to let go, she would have. But that was impossible now. The only thing she could do was reach up and try to pry the viselike fingers from her shoulder. But she hadn't counted on the way his warm flesh would feel under her own. The gesture, which had started as a desperate bid for escape, ended as a caress. God, it was good to touch him after so long, she thought, unable to keep from pressing the lengths of her fingers against the slightly hair-roughened backs of his and then moving down to stroke his knuckles.

It took a few seconds to realize that he had turned his hand palm-up and stilled the movement of her fingers with a steady grip. And then, suddenly, his arms were around her shoulders, pulling her against the wall of his chest and holding her close.

"Sarah," he breathed, his own voice so thick with emotion that he could hardly manage the two syllables. She felt his arms around her back and his hands pressing into her shoulders. It felt so good to be in his arms again, if only for a little while.

Her knees were too weak to support her now. And so she was forced to cling to him to keep her balance. It would only be for a moment, she told herself. And then she would find the strength to leave. But the moment seemed to stretch between them. She couldn't keep from pressing her face against his shirt front, feeling the warmth of his body, taking in his clean male scent mixed with the aftershave lotion she had noticed earlier. She wanted to reach up and find the tapered hair at the back of his neck and brush her fingers against it. But that would be too much of a liberty, she knew. And so she simply stood there, trying to marshal the resolve to walk out of his life.

As though from a long distance away, she heard him ask again, *"Why* did you come here?"

This time the question was confusing to her brain— befogged by strong emotion and physical contact with Matt. But if there was anything she knew, it was why she had come. "Because I love you," she whispered, only half-realizing that she had actually spoken the words aloud.

Yet Matt heard. "Sarah, oh, Sarah," he groaned, his lips against her hair. "I never thought I'd hear you say that." If it were possible, his arms tightened around her back, pulling her closer. He seemed to be clinging to her for strength, just as she was clinging to him.

Then, to her bewilderment, she felt him lift her off the floor and shift her weight so that he held her with one arm under her knees and the other around her shoulder. Turning, he strode back down the hall to his studio, pausing to pull the door shut after he had crossed the threshold. They were in the reception area that led to the screening room, Sarah realized dimly. But instead of opening the door behind the desk, Matt crossed to one opposite, which stood ajar. On the other side was a tastefully furnished living room, although she barely took it in. Sitting down on a brown velvet sofa, Matt brought Sarah along with him and settled her on his lap.

For an endless moment he held her cradled tightly against himself, until finally Sarah could sense the tension gradually seeping out of his body. She felt his cheek, then, press gently against hers before he began to move his head in a slow, caressing circle, the way he had that first time in her studio when he hadn't wanted to get the clay from his hands on her.

It was a simple gesture. And yet it said so much. Sarah felt something inside her chest contract. Wordlessly, she

181

reached up now to bury her fingers in the thickness of his hair as she had longed to do in the hall. And then, as though a dam of emotion had burst inside him, he turned, his lips seeking hers in a kiss that demanded confirmation of what had just happened between them in the hall.

The unbridled passion of it left them both breathless. And for several heartbeats they simply clung together. But Sarah knew there was so much to be said between them.

"Matt," she whispered, her lips only inches from his. "I was afraid to love you, afraid of what would happen when . . . when you finally left me."

Her words brought a grimace of anguish to Matt's features. "Sarah, I wasn't going to leave you. I love you. I think I started loving you that first morning on the beach when I carried Eustace home. But I knew you were afraid to let anyone get close to you."

The insight made her squeeze her eyes shut as Matt continued, his voice filled with self-deprecation now. "I thought I was finally getting somewhere with you when that damn letter from your sister arrived and made you think I was just out to use you. Suddenly I was back to nowhere with you—less than nowhere. I had to win your trust all over again. But after the way we made love that night before I was coming back down here, I thought it was finally safe to let you know how I really felt. When I told you I loved you that morning and you treated it like it was some kind of joke—"

Sarah stopped him from continuing with a soft little kiss. "Don't," she murmured, her lips moving against his as she spoke. "I couldn't let myself believe that you truly cared for me."

Matt nodded. "I know that now. But, Sarah, when you sent me away to New York, it was as if the world had come to an end. During the day I could keep myself from thinking about how miserable I was by working. But the nights, Sarah, the nights. Tonight was about the worst. I was trying to make myself get dressed to go to a screening a friend was having, but I couldn't keep my mind on what I was doing. If you hadn't knocked on the door, I think I would have left the apartment without my shoes on."

Sarah nodded. "It was like that for me, too. But I couldn't even work. If I hadn't had most of the pieces for my show done before you left, there wouldn't have been any show."

Matt reached down to stroke her face again as if assuring himself that she was not some happy illusion his brain had conjured up. "I lay awake in bed thinking of you, aching for you," he whispered. "That last wonderful night we had together played over and over again in my mind. But it was a painful mockery because I wondered if you'd ever let me make love to you again," he said, clasping her passionately against himself. "It's been hell without you, and I need you now, Sarah."

Sarah clung to him, knowing that what he wanted so desperately was what she wanted, too. If only her doubts and fears had not marred their relationship from the first. Was there some way of making up to Matt for that? Was there some way of showing Matt just how much she trusted him with her most intimate emotions now?

And suddenly, she knew there was.

"Lie down, Matt," she whispered, moving off his lap and perching on the edge of the sofa.

He raised a questioning eyebrow.

Suddenly she grinned wickedly. "I want you to be comfortable."

"Comfortable for what?" he questioned, his expression quizzical.

"You have to lie down to find out."

Willing to indulge her almost anything tonight, he obeyed.

"Are you comfortable?" she asked.

He nodded, lacing his fingers together behind his head

Sarah leaned over then and brushed her lips lightly against his before her tongue darted out to tease his mouth open and then gently explore the inner surface of his lips. When he began to respond in kind, she withdrew slightly.

"No, let me do it," she urged. "Let me make love to you."

His eyes widened, but he said nothing. Accepting his silence as acquiescence, she took his lower lip between her teeth, gently nibbling on it before doing the same with the top one. She heard and felt his indrawn breath and knew the heady sense of sexual excitement that giving pleasure brings. In the next moment, she claimed his mouth, exploring and seeking, finding and bestowing.

At the same time, her hands were not idle. They had found the buttons of his shirt and were busy slipping them open. Sarah's mouth left Matt's to string little kisses along his jaw and neck. Pushing the edges of his shirt aside, she pressed her cheek against the muscled wall of his chest and then turned her head to find one male nipple with her tongue and lips.

"Ah, Sarah," she heard him groan, feeling her own nipples harden as though he were the active partner and not the other way around.

Drawing back slightly, she removed first one arm and then the other from behind his head so that she could undo the cuffs before helping him take the shirt off.

Then, standing up, she looked down at him for a moment, wanting to press herself against his magnificently naked torso. But not yet, not yet.

First she slowly removed her shoes, realizing that she was stalling for time. She knew exactly what she wanted to do now. But it depended on making a sensual performance out of taking off her clothes. Was there a sexy way to get out of panty hose? she wondered. She'd just have to see. Turning slightly, she reached down to unroll one leg of the black, open-work garment, smiling slightly at Matt over her shoulder. Then, angling her body so that he could see her foot and part of her leg, she took her time with the other leg, noting with satisfaction the way Matt's smoldering gaze followed the progress.

When she had shed the panty hose, Sarah turned all the way toward the man on the couch who was watching her now with heart-stopping intensity. Deliberately she took a step back to give him a better view. And then, her eyes never leaving his, she reached for the zipper at the back of her aqua dinner dress and began to lower it inch by inch. His sharp indrawn breath as she freed her arms from the cap sleeves and let the dress fall gracefully around her ankles made her shiver. It was all she could do to keep from rushing back to his arms. And yet, and yet . . . she knew how much better it would be if she waited.

Clad in only her panties, half-slip, and bra, Sarah smiled tantalizingly down at Matt for a moment. Then she quickly sent the slip to join the aqua dress.

She saw his knuckles whiten in a tight grip on the edge of the sofa as she reached languidly around to unclasp her bra. And for a moment her fingers, made clumsy by her own rising need, fumbled with the fastening. As she dropped the bra, she felt his now burning gaze stroke and caress her breasts, making them ache for a more substantial touch.

She knew her heart was pounding wildly inside her chest as she hooked her fingers under the edge of her lacy panties and pulled them down over her thighs. When she stepped out of this last remaining garment, her name was on Matt's lips like a strangled cry.

Though every fiber of her being drew her toward him now, she forced herself to wait. With slow deliberation she cupped her hands under her breasts, lifting them tantalizingly toward Matt. The sexual invitation in the gesture was too much for him to take lying down. Before she quite realized what was happening, he had sprung off the couch and closed the short distance between them. His arms were steel bands as he hauled her naked body tightly against himself. The feel of her breasts against his chest at last was overwhelming. And when his hands slid down her silky flanks to press her hips against his own, she knew for a certainty just how effectively she had aroused him.

"I ought to paddle your bottom, you little witch," he growled, his breath fanning her ear. "But I have a better idea."

She felt herself lifted from the floor then. And in a moment she was being carried across the rug and through a doorway into Matt's bedroom.

Reaching down with one arm, he threw back the covers and deposited her on the wide bed before quickly dispatching the rest of his clothing. And then he was covering her soft body with the length of his hard one.

Although they had hardly touched, Sarah's teasing little performance had inflamed them both almost beyond endurance. Each understood the other's unquenched desire—not just for physical release but for an end to their emotional estrangement. Each sought that most intimate of joining now with an almost savage fierceness. And when it was accomplished, they began to move together urgently, giving and receiving in a frenzy of passion which quickly spiraled up and up and out of control. The tempestuous explosion came quickly, leaving them clinging to each other in wonder at what had just happened between them.

For a long moment after it was over, neither moved. And then Matt shifted his weight slightly so that he could reach up to trail his fingers gently along Sarah's cheek and then her lips. At the feather-light touch they parted slightly and she kissed his fingertips before beginning to nibble at them delicately.

Matt smiled fondly down at her, secure at last in the knowledge that she was finally his.

As if mirroring his thoughts, she began to speak, her

186

breath a caress where her mouth had wet his fingers. "I'm not afraid anymore," she whispered.

"Afraid?"

"To belong to you. To know that you belong to me." Her face clouded slightly as she hurried on. "I almost ruined it, you know—because I was so frightened of just opening up and giving."

Matt's fingertips stilled her lips. "Don't," he ordered. "Don't blame yourself. I'm the one who should have been straight with you from the beginning. We both know that's the truth."

"But—" Sarah tried again.

This time Matt silenced her with his mouth, first kissing her and then beginning to nibble at her lips as she had done with his fingers. It was an effective tactic.

"You always could get around me like that." Sarah sighed. "Even when I told myself I couldn't trust you.

"You mean after the letter from your sister, don't you? Matt questioned.

She nodded. It was a painful subject for both of them. Instead of speaking, Matt rolled to his side and pulled Sarah tightly against his body, letting her know without words just how much losing her would have cost him.

"I thought I'd let you slip away from me, Sarah," he finally admitted huskily. "That's why I went by to see your show before it opened, so I could buy that mysterious piece you wouldn't let me see. I knew it was something that meant a great deal to you and I wanted it. When I saw *Dream Woman*, I knew it would be the closest thing to having you."

Sarah's eyes widened. "*You're* the one who bought it. Mr. Vasholz couldn't tell me who it was."

"Actually, those were the instructions I gave him. I didn't want you to find out."

Sarah squeezed her eyes shut and pressed her forehead

187

against his shoulder. "Oh, Matt," she murmured. "If I'd known . . ."

"Well, it's okay now—now that I know you're going to marry me."

"I'm going to *what?*" Sarah questioned, sitting up and looking at him in disbelief.

"Marry me. Have my children. Share my fondest hopes and dreams. Or didn't you know where all this was leading?"

"I guess I hadn't gotten that far," she admitted, unable now to repress a silly grin.

Matt pressed his advantage. "We're going to share something that few couples do. We're not just great in bed together, you know." It was his turn to grin as he enjoyed the flush that spread across her face and down her neck. "Your influence has done something fantastic for my work. When I asked for your cooperation with *The Wallace Kiteredge Story,* I told myself that I didn't really need your help—that I could do just as good a job without you, if things didn't work out."

Sarah opened her mouth to speak. But Matt hurried on. "That isn't how things turned out at all. Sharing the project with you brought out something in me I didn't even know existed. There's a life, a spirit to that film that I couldn't have achieved without you."

Sarah nodded, knowing exactly what he meant. "It was the same with *Dream Woman,*" she admitted. "I didn't realize it at the time, but it was your influence that brought out what I was trying to achieve with that piece of sculpture. Before you walked—or ran—into my life, I just couldn't get her right."

Matt reached up to pull the woman he loved down beside him on the bed again. Turning toward her, he brushed back a wayward strand of her dark hair. For a moment neither spoke. And yet Sarah knew there was something more that had to be said.

"Matt, what you're talking about is what my father never had with my mother—what he had to find with someone else—with Marjorie Winter."

She felt his arm tighten on her shoulder. But she shook her head. "No, it's all right," she murmured. "I know it's true. And you're the one who made me see it."

"Sarah," he breathed. "We're going to give each other everything two people can give to one another." And then he drew back to look into her eyes. She expected a serious expression on his face. But, instead, his own green eyes were twinkling.

"What exactly is so amusing?" she questioned.

"Oh, I was just thinking how we'll tell our children that a dragon named Eustace brought us together. Do you think he's going to be handed down in our family for generations to come? Because I know we're going to give each other children. And with our artistic talents, our kids should be fantastic," he ended huskily.

"Matt!"

"And since the future Mrs. Lyons is already an old lady of thirty-two, I think we should get started rather quickly, don't you?" he added with mock seriousness.

Sarah squeaked as he made his immediate intentions very clear. But he stopped her protest with his lips and for several heartbeats their attentions were fully with each other.

"Besides," Matt finally murmured, "if you won't let me have my wicked way with you, I can always use blackmail if I have to."

Sarah raised an inquisitive eyebrow.

"How would you like me to tell the critics just who modeled for that naked statue in the Vasholz Gallery?"

"You wouldn't," Sarah sputtered, before calling his bluff. "And just how do you know who it is, anyway?"

"How could I not know?" he retorted, cupping one creamy breast with his hand and then trailing his fingers seductively down her rib cage and then to her thigh. "I know the lovely model too well. But I'd actually prefer to keep the secret to myself, you know. I wouldn't want every cabdriver in New York knowing what my wife looks like in the all together."

The touch made Sarah sigh with pleasure. And then, all at once, her body stiffened. "Cabdriver!" she groaned.

"What is it?" Matt questioned. "Did I go too far this time?"

Sarah shook her head. "No, this is all my fault. When I came up here, I didn't know if you'd be home. So I told the cabdriver to wait. He's still waiting!"

Matt threw back his head and laughed. "I guess it's flattering to realize just how much I have you in my thrall, except for the small fortune involved. I'd better get dressed and go down there. But I expect some sort of reward when I come back."

Sarah nodded contritely. "Yes, my lord," she murmured. "I will have something special planned, I promise." And then she grinned impishly. "And it won't be a pan full of burned muffins."

Matt grinned back. "That's a relief. In fact, if you ever get the impulse to make muffins, stifle it. I'd rather see your creativity come out in other ways."

Sarah knew exactly what he meant.

LOOK FOR NEXT MONTH'S
CANDLELIGHT ECSTASY ROMANCES ®